W9-CLQ-231

It wouldn't hurt to pretend for one night, would it?

Careful not to disturb her, he gently slid his arms beneath her and, quilt and all, carried her to his bed. When she was safely tucked into one side, he crossed to the other, stripped down and stretched out beneath the sheets.

Lying flat on his back, he tipped his head her way. The black gloss of hair was all he could see above the quilt, but the series of lumps beneath it suggested far more.

Eyes rising to the darkened rafters, he shifted once, paused, then shifted again. With each shift, he inched closer to her. He couldn't feel her warmth, couldn't smell her scent. Multiple layers of bedclothes plus a safe twelve inches of space prevented that. But he knew she was there, and in the dark, where no one could see or know, he smiled.

"Barbara Delinsky continues to be a powerhouse figure in mainstream fiction."
—*Romantic Times BOOKclub*

BARBARA DELINSKY

Twelve Across

MIRA®

If you purchased this book without a cover you should be aware
that this book is stolen property. It was reported as "unsold and
destroyed" to the publisher, and neither the author nor the
publisher has received any payment for this "stripped book."

ISBN 0-7783-2385-4

TWELVE ACROSS

Copyright © 1987 by Barbara Delinsky.

All rights reserved. Except for use in any review, the reproduction or
utilization of this work in whole or in part in any form by any electronic,
mechanical or other means, now known or hereafter invented, including
xerography, photocopying and recording, or in any information storage or
retrieval system, is forbidden without the written permission of the publisher,
MIRA Books, 225 Duncan Mill Road, Don Mills, Ontario, Canada M3B 3K9.

All characters in this book have no existence outside the imagination of the
author and have no relation whatsoever to anyone bearing the same name
or names. They are not even distantly inspired by any individual known or
unknown to the author, and all incidents are pure invention.

MIRA and the Star Colophon are trademarks used under license and registered
in Australia, New Zealand, Philippines, United States Patent and Trademark
Office and in other countries.

www.MIRABooks.com

Printed in U.S.A.

Twelve Across

1

Leah Gates made a final fold in the blue foil paper, then studied her creation in dismay. "This does not look like a roadrunner," she whispered to the woman at the table beside her.

Victoria Lesser, who'd been diligently folding a pelican, shifted her attention to her friend's work. "Sure, it does," she whispered back. "It's a roadrunner."

"And I'm a groundhog." Leah raised large, round glasses from the bridge of her nose in the hope that a myopic view would improve the image. It didn't. She dropped the frames back into place.

"It's a roadrunner," Victoria repeated.

"You're squinting."

"It looks like a roadrunner."

"It looks like a conglomeration of pointed paper prongs."

Lifting the fragile item, Victoria turned it from side to side. She had to agree with Leah's assessment, though she was far too tactful to say so. "Did you get the stretched bird base right?"

"I thought so."

"And the book fold and the mountain fold?"

"As far as I know."

"Then there must be some problem with the rabbit-ear fold."

"I think the problem's with me."

"Nuh-uh."

"Then with you," Leah scolded in the same hushed whisper. "It was your idea to take an origami course. How do I let myself get talked into these things?"

"Very easily. You love them as much as I do. Besides, you're a puzzle solver, and what's origami but a puzzle in paper? You've done fine up to now. So today's an off day."

"That's an understatement," Leah muttered.

"Ladies?" came a call from the front of the room. Both Leah and Victoria looked up to find the instructor's reproving stare homing in on them over the heads of the other students. "I believe we're ready to start on the frog base. Are there any final questions on the stretched bird base?"

Leah quickly shook her head, then bit her lip against a moan of despair. The frog base?

Victoria simply sat with a gentle smile on her face. By the time the class had ended, though, the smile had faded. Taking Leah by the arm, she ushered her toward the door. "Come on," she said softly. "Let's get some coffee."

When they were seated in a small coffee shop on Third Avenue, Victoria wasted no time in speaking her mind. "Something's bothering you. Out with it."

Leah set her glasses on the table. They'd fogged up the instant she'd come in from the cold, and long-time experience told her they'd be useless for several minutes. The oversize fuchsia sweater Victoria wore was more than bright enough to be seen by the weakest of eyes, however, and above the sweater was the gentlest of expressions. It was toward these that Leah sent a sheepish look. "My frog base stunk, too, huh?"

"Your mind wasn't on it. Your attention's been elsewhere all night. Where, if I may be so bold as to ask?"

Leah had to laugh at that. In the year she'd known Victoria Lesser, the woman had on occasion been far bolder. But not once had Leah minded. What might have been considered intrusive in others was caring in Victoria. She was compassionate, down-to-earth and insightful, and had such a remarkably positive view of the world that time spent with her was always uplifting.

"Guess," Leah invited with a wry half grin.

"Well, I know your mind's not on your marriage, because that's been over and done for two years now. And I know it's not on a man, because despite my own considerable—" she drawled the word pointedly "—efforts to fix you up, you refuse to date. And I doubt it's on your work, because crosswords are in as much of a demand as ever, and because just last week you told me that your contract's been renewed. Which leaves your apartment." Victoria knew how much Leah adored the loft she'd lived in since her divorce. "Is your landlord raising the rent?"

"Worse."

"Oh-oh. He's talking condo conversion."

"He's *decided* condo conversion."

"Oh, sweetheart. Mucho?"

"Mucho mucho."

"When's it happening?"

"Too soon." Idly Leah strummed the rim of her glasses, then, as though recalling their purpose, slipped them back onto her nose. "I can look for another place, but I doubt I'll find one half as nice. Waterfront buildings are hot, and most of them have already gone condo. Even if there were a vacancy in one of the few remaining rentals, I doubt I could afford it."

"Thank you, New York."

"Mmm." Seeking to warm her chilled fingers, Leah wrapped her hands around her coffee cup. "Prices have gone sky-high in the two years since I rented the loft. The only reason I got it at a reasonable rate in the first place was that I was willing to fix it up myself. It was a mess when I first saw it, but the view was…ineffable."

"Ineffable?"

"Indescribable. It isn't fair, Victoria. For weeks I scraped walls and ceilings, sanded, painted, and now someone else will reap the fruits of my labor." She gave a frustrated growl. "I had a feeling this was coming, but that doesn't make it any easier to take."

Victoria's heart went out to this woman who'd become such a special friend. They'd met the year before in the public library and had hit it off from the start. Victoria had enjoyed Leah's subtle wit and soft-spoken manner. Though at the age of thirty-three Leah was twenty years younger, they shared an interest in things new and different. They'd gone to the theater together, tried out newly opened restaurants together, taken classes not only in origami but in papier-mâché, conversational Russian and ballet.

Victoria had come to know Leah well. She'd learned that Leah had been badly burned by an unhappy mar-

riage and that behind the urban adventuress was a ba-
sically shy woman. She also saw that Leah had con-
structed a very tidy and self-contained shell for herself,
and that within that shell was a world of loneliness and
vulnerability. Losing the apartment she loved would
feed that vulnerability.

"You know," Victoria ventured, "I'd be more
than happy to loan you the down payment on that
condo—"

The hand Leah pressed over hers cut off her words.
"I can't take your money."

"But I have it. More than enough—"

"It's not my way, Victoria. I wouldn't be comfortable. And it's not as much a matter of principle as it is
the amount of money involved. If I had to make loan
payments to you on top of mortgage payments to the
bank, I'd be house-poor. Another few years… That's all
I'd have needed to save for the down payment myself."
It might have taken less if she'd been more frugal, but
Leah lived comfortably and enjoyed it. She took pleasure in splurging on an exquisite hand-knit sweater, a
pair of imported shoes, a piece of original art. She reasoned that she'd earned them. But a bank wouldn't take
them as collateral. "Unfortunately I don't have another
few years."

"You wouldn't have to pay me back right away."

"That's bad business."

"So? It's my money, my business—"

"And our friendship. I'd feel awkward taking advantage of it."

"I'm the one who's made the offer. There'd be no
taking advantage involved."

But Leah was shaking her head. "Thanks, but I can't. I just can't."

Victoria opened her mouth to speak, then paused. She'd been about to suggest that Richard might help. Given the fact that Leah had been married to him once and that she had no other family, it seemed the only other option. He had money. Unfortunately he also had a new wife and a child. Victoria knew that Leah's pride wouldn't allow her to ask him for a thing. "What will you do?"

"Look for another place, I guess. If I have to settle for something less exciting, so be it."

"Are you sure you want to stay in the city? Seems to me you could get a super place somewhere farther out."

Leah considered that idea. "But I like the city."

"You're used to the city. You've lived here all your life. Maybe it's time for a change."

"I don't know—"

"It'd be good for you, sweetheart. New scenery, new people, new stores, new courses—"

"Are you trying to get rid of me?"

"And lose my companion in whimsy? Of course not! But I'd be selfish if I didn't encourage you to spread your wings a little. One part of you loves new experiences. The other part avoids them. But you're young, Leah. You have so much living to do."

"What better place to do it than here? I mean, if New York isn't multifarious—"

"Leah, please."

"Diverse, as in filled with opportunities, okay? If New York isn't that, what place is?"

"Just about any place. Perhaps it'd be a different

kind of experience…" The wheels in Victoria's mind were beginning to turn. "You know, there's another possibility entirely. If you were willing to shift gears, if you were game…" She shook her head. "No. Maybe not."

"What?"

"It'd be too much. Forget I mentioned it."

"You haven't mentioned anything," Leah pointed out in her quiet way. But she was curious, just as she was sure Victoria had intended. "What were you thinking of?"

It was a minute before Victoria answered, and the delay wasn't all for effect. She hated to be devious with someone she adored as much as she did Leah. And yet…and yet…it could possibly work. Hadn't a little deviousness brought two other good friends of hers together?

"I have a place. It's pretty secluded."

"The island in Maine?"

"There's that, but it wasn't what I had in mind." The island was totally secluded. She didn't want Leah to be alone; that would defeat the purpose. "I have a cabin in New Hampshire. Arthur bought it years ago as a hunting lodge. I've been up several times since he died, but it's a little too quiet for me." She shook her head again. "No. It'd be too quiet for you, too. You're used to the city."

"Tell me more."

"You like the city."

"Tell me, Victoria."

Again Victoria paused, this time entirely for effect. "It's in the middle of the woods, and it's small," she said with caution.

"Go on."

"We're talking mountain retreat here."

"Yes."

"There are two rooms—a living area and a bedroom. The nearest town is three miles away. You'd hate it, Leah."

But Leah wasn't so sure. She was intimidated by the idea of moving to a suburban neighborhood, but something rustic… It was a new thought, suddenly worth considering. "I don't know as I could buy it."

"It's not for sale," Victoria said quickly. "But I could easily loan—"

"Rent. It'd have to be a rental."

"Okay. I could easily rent it to you for a little while. That's all you'd need to decide whether you can live outside New York. You could view it as a trial run."

"Are there people nearby?"

"In the town, yes. Not many, mind you, and they're quiet, private types."

So much the better, Leah thought. She didn't care to cope with throngs of new faces. "That's okay. I could do my work at a mountain cabin without any problem, and if I had books and a tape deck—"

"There's a community of artists about fifteen miles from the mountain. You once mentioned wanting to learn how to weave. You'd have the perfect opportunity for that." Victoria considered mentioning Garrick, then ruled against it for the time being. Leah was smiling; she obviously liked what she'd heard so far. It seemed that reverse psychology was the way to go. "It's not New York," she reminded her friend gently.

"I know."

"It'd be a total change."

"I know."

"A few minutes ago you said you didn't want to leave New York."

"But my apartment's being stolen from under me, so some change is inevitable."

"You could still look for another apartment."

"I could."

"Or move to the suburbs."

Leah's firm head shake sent thick black hair shimmering along the crew neckline of her sweater.

"I want you to think about this, Leah. It'd be a pretty drastic step."

"True, but not an irrevocable one. If I'm climbing the walls after a week, I can turn around and come back. I really wouldn't be any worse off than I am now, would I?" She didn't wait for Victoria to answer. She was feeling more enthused than she had since she'd learned she was losing her loft. "Tell me more about the cabin itself. Is it primitive?"

Victoria laughed. "If you'd had a chance to know Arthur, you'd have the answer to that. Arthur Lesser never did anything primitive. For that matter, you know me. I'm not exactly the rough-it-in-the-wild type, am I?"

Leah had spent time in Victoria's Park Avenue co-op. It was spacious, stylish, sumptuous. She'd also seen her plush summer place in the Hamptons. But neither Manhattan nor Long Island was a secluded mountain in New Hampshire, and for all her wealth, Victoria wasn't snobbish. She was just enough of a nonconformist to survive for a stretch on the bare basics.

Leah, who'd never had the kind of wealth that inspired total nonconformity, liked to go into things with her eyes open. "Is the cabin well equipped?"

"When last I saw it, it was," Victoria said with an innocence that concealed a multitude of sins. "Don't make a decision now, sweetheart. Think about it for a bit. If you decide to go up there, you'd have to store your furniture. I don't know how you feel about that."

"It shouldn't be difficult."

"It'd be a pain in the neck."

"Being ousted from my apartment is a pain in the neck. If movers have to come in, what difference does it make where they take my things? Besides, if I hate it in New Hampshire, I won't have to worry about my furniture while I look around back here for a place to live."

"The green room's yours if you want it."

Leah grinned. While she'd never have taken a monetary loan, the use of that beautiful room in Victoria's apartment, where she'd already spent a night or two on occasion, was a security blanket she'd welcome. "I was hoping you'd say that."

"Well, you'd better remember it. I'd never forgive myself if, after I talked you into it, you hated the mountains and then didn't have anywhere to turn." Actually, Victoria was more worried that Leah would be the one without forgiveness. But it was a risk worth taking. Victoria had gone with her instincts where Deirdre and Neil Hersey were concerned, and things couldn't have worked out better. Now here was Leah—tall and slender, adorable with her glossy black page boy and bangs, and her huge round glasses with thin red frames. If Leah could meet Garrick...

"I'll take it," Leah was saying.

"The green room? Of course you will."

"No, the cabin. I'll take the cabin." Leah wasn't an impulsive person, but she did know her own mind. When something appealed to her, she saw no point in waffling. Victoria's mountain retreat sounded like a perfect solution to the problem she'd been grappling with for seventy-two hours straight. It would afford her the time to think things through and decide where to go from there. "Just tell me how much you want for rent."

Victoria brushed the matter aside with the graceful wave of one hand. "No rush on that. We can discuss it later."

"I'm paying rent, Victoria. If you don't let me, the deal's off."

"I agreed that you could pay rent, sweetheart. It's just that I have no idea how much to charge. Why don't you see what shape things are in when you get there? Then you can pay me whatever you think the place merits."

"I'd rather pay you in advance."

"And I'd rather wait."

"You're being pertinacious."

Victoria wasn't sure what "pertinacious" meant, but she could guess. "That's right."

"Fine. I'll wait as you've asked, but so help me, Victoria, if you return my check—"

"I won't," Victoria said, fully confident that it wouldn't come to that. "Have faith, Leah. Have faith."

Leah had faith. It grew day by day, along with her enthusiasm. She surprised herself at times, because she truly was a dyed-in-the-wool urbanite. Yet something about an abrupt change in life-style appealed to her for the very first time. She wondered if it had something to do with her age; perhaps the thirties brought boldness. Or desperation. No, she didn't want to think that. Perhaps she was simply staging a belated rebellion against the way of life she'd known from birth.

It had been years since she'd taken a vacation, much less one to a remote spot. She remembered short jaunts to Cape Cod with her parents, when she'd been a child and remote had consisted of isolated sand dunes and sunrise sails. The trips she'd taken with her husband had never been remote in any sense. Inevitably they'd been tied to his work, and she'd found them far from relaxing. Richard had been constantly *on,* which wouldn't have bothered her if he hadn't been so fussy about how she looked and behaved when she was by his side. Not that she'd given him cause for complaint; she'd been born and bred in the urban arena and knew how to play its games when necessary. Unfortunately Richard's games had incorporated rules she hadn't anticipated.

But Leah wasn't thinking about Richard on the day in late March when she left Manhattan. She was thinking of the gut instinct that told her she was doing the right thing. And she was thinking of the farewell dinner Victoria had insisted on treating her to the night before.

They'd spent the better part of the meal chatting about incidentals. Only when they'd reached dessert did they get around to the nitty-gritty. "You're all set to go, then?"

"You bet."

Victoria had had many a qualm in the three weeks since she'd suggested the plan, and in truth, she was feeling a little like a weasel. It was fine and dandy, she knew, to say that she had Leah's best interests at heart. She was still being manipulative, and Leah was bound to be angry when she discovered the fact. "Are you sure you want to go through with this?"

"Uh-huh."

"There isn't any air-conditioning."

"In the mountains? I should hope not."

"Or phone."

"So you've told me," Leah said with a smile. "Twice. I'll give you a call from town once I'm settled."

Victoria wasn't sure whether to look forward to that or not. "Did the storage people get all your furniture?"

"This morning."

"My Lord, that means the bed, too! Where will you sleep tonight?"

"On the floor. And no, I don't want the green room. I've about had it with packing. Everything's ready to go from my place. All I'll have to do in the morning is load up the car and take off."

A night on the bare floor. Victoria felt guiltier than ever, but she knew a stubborn expression when she saw one. "Is the car okay?"

It was a demo Volkswagen Golf that Leah had bought from a dealer three days before. "The car is fine."

"Can you drive it?"

"Sure can."

"You haven't driven in years, Leah."

"It's like riding a bike—you never forget how. Isn't that what you told me two weeks ago? Come on, Victoria. It's not like you to be a worrywart."

She was right. Still, Victoria felt uncomfortable. With

Deirdre and Neil, there had been a single phone call from each and they'd been on their way. With Leah it had meant three weeks of deception, which seemed to make the crime that much greater.

But what was done was done. Leah's mind was set. Her arrangements were made. She was going.

Taking a deep breath, Victoria produced first a reassuring smile, then two envelopes from her purse. "Directions to the cabin," she said, handing over the top one. "I had my secretary type them up, and they're quite detailed." Cautiously she watched Leah remove the paper and scan it. She knew the exact moment Leah reached the instructions on the bottom, and responded to her frown by explaining, "Garrick Rodenhiser is a trapper. His cabin is several miles from mine by car, but there's an old logging trail through the woods that will get you there on foot in no time. In case of emergency you're to contact him. He's a good man. He'll help you in any way he can."

"Goodness," Leah murmured distractedly as she reread the directions, "you sound as though you expect trouble."

"Nonsense. But I do trust Garrick. When I'm up there alone myself, it's a comfort knowing he's around."

"Well—" Leah folded the paper and returned it to the envelope "—I'm sure I'll be fine."

"So you will be," Victoria declared, holding out the second envelope. "For Garrick. Deliver it for me?"

Leah took it, then turned it over and over. It was sealed and opaque, with the trapper's name written on the front in Victoria's elegant script. "A love letter?" she teased, tapping the tip of the envelope against her nose.

"Somehow I can't imagine you with a craggy old trapper."

"Craggy old trappers can be very nice."

"Are there lots of them up there?"

"A few."

"Don't they smell?"

Victoria laughed. "That's precious, Leah."

"They don't?"

"Not badly."

"Oh. Okay. Well, that's good. Y'know, this trip could well be educational."

That was, in many ways, how Leah thought of it as she worked her way through the midtown traffic. The car was packed to the hilt with clothing and other essentials, boxes of books, a tape deck and three cases of cassettes, plus sundry supplies. She had dozens of plans, projects to keep her busy over and above the crossword puzzles she intended to create.

Filling her mind with these prospects was in part a defense mechanism, she knew, and it was successful only to a point. There remained a certain wistfulness in leaving the loft where she'd been independent for the first time in her life, saying goodbye to the little man at the corner kiosk from whom she'd bought the *Times* each day, bidding a silent farewell to the theaters and restaurants and museums she wouldn't be visiting for a while.

The exhaust fumes that surrounded her were as familiar as the traffic. Not so the sense of nostalgia that assailed her as she navigated the Golf through the streets. She'd loved New York from the time she'd been old enough to appreciate it as a city. Her parents' apartment had been modest by New York standards, but Central Park had been free to all, as had Fifth Avenue, Rockefeller Center and Washington Square.

Memories. A few close friends. The kind of anonymity she liked. Such was New York. But they'd all be there when she returned. Determinedly squaring her shoulders, she thrust off sentimentality in favor of practicality, which at the moment meant avoiding swerving taxis and swarming pedestrians as she headed toward the East River.

Traffic was surprisingly heavy for ten in the morning, and Leah was the kind of driver others either loved or hated. When in doubt she yielded the road, which meant grins on the faces of those who cut her off and impatient honks from those behind her. She was relieved to leave the concrete jungle behind and start north on the thruway.

It was a sunny day, mild for March, a good omen, she decided. Though she'd brought heavier clothes with her, she was glad she'd worn a pair of lightweight knit pants and a loose cashmere sweater for the drive. She was comfortable and increasingly relaxed as she coasted in the limbo between city and country.

By the time she reached the outskirts of Boston, it was two o'clock and she was famished. As eager to stretch as to eat, she pulled into a Burger King on the turnpike and climbed from the car, pausing only to grab for her jacket before heading for the restaurant. The sun was lost behind cloud cover that had gathered since she'd reached the Massachusetts border, and the air had grown chilly. Knowing that she had another three hours of driving before her, and desperately wanting to reach the cabin before dark, she gulped down a burger and a Coke, used the rest rooms, then was quickly on her way again.

The sky darkened progressively. With the New Hampshire border came a light drizzle. So much for good omens, she mused silently as she turned one switch after another until at last she hit paydirt with the windshield wipers. Within half an hour she set them to swishing double time.

It was pouring. Dark, gloomy, cold and wet. Leah thanked her lucky stars that she'd read the directions so many times before she'd left, because she loathed the idea of pulling over to the side of the road even for the briefest of moments. With the typed words neatly etched in her brain, she was able to devote her full concentration to driving.

And driving demanded it. She eased up on the gas, but even then had to struggle to see the road through the torrent. Lane markers were sadly blurred. The back spray from passing cars made the already poor visibility worse. She breathed a sigh of relief when she found her turnoff, then tensed up again when the sudden sparsity of other cars meant the absence of taillights as guides.

But she drove on. She passed a restaurant and briefly considered taking shelter until the storm was spent, but decided that it would be far worse to have to negotiate strange roads—and a lonesome cabin—in the dark later. She passed a dingy motel and toyed with the idea of taking a room for the night, but decided that she really did want to be in the cabin. Having left behind the life she'd always known, she was feeling unsettled; spending the night in a fleabag motel wouldn't help.

What would help, she decided grimly, would be an end to the rain. And a little sun peeking through the clouds. And several extra hours of daylight.

None of those happened. The rain did lessen to a steady downpour, but the sky grew darker and darker as daylight began to wane. The fiddling she'd done earlier in search of the wipers paid off; she knew just what to press to turn on the headlights.

When she passed through the small town Victoria had mentioned, she was elated. Elation faded in an instant, though, when she took the prescribed turn past the post office and saw what lay ahead.

A narrow, twisting road, barely wide enough for two cars. No streetlamps. No center line. No directional signs.

Leah sat ramrod straight at the wheel. Her knuckles were white, her eyes straining to delineate the rain-spattered landscape ahead. Too late she realized that she hadn't checked the odometer when she'd passed the post office. One-point-nine miles to the turnoff, her instructions said. How far had she gone? All but creeping along the uphill grade, she searched for the triangular boulder backed by a stand of twisted birch that would mark the start of Victoria's road.

It was just another puzzle, Leah told herself. She loved puzzles.

She hated this one. If she missed the road... But she didn't want to miss the road. One-point-nine miles at fifteen miles an hour...eight minutes... How long had she been driving since she'd left the town?

Just when she was about to stop and return to the post office to take an odometer reading, she saw a triangular boulder backed by a stand of twisted birch. And a road. Vaguely.

It was with mixed feelings that she made the turn, for not only was she suddenly on rutted dirt, but forested growth closed in on her, slapping the sides of the car. In her anxious state it sounded clearly hostile.

She began to speak to herself, albeit silently. *This is God's land, Leah. The wild and woolly outdoors. Picture it in the bright sunshine. You'll love it.*

The car bumped and jerked along, jolting her up and down and from side to side. One of the tires began to spin and she caught her breath, barely releasing it when the car surged onward and upward. The words she spoke to herself grew more beseechful. *Just a little farther, Leah. You're almost there. Come on, Golf, don't fade on me now.*

Her progress was agonizingly slow, made all the more so by the steepening pitch as the road climbed the hill. The Golf didn't falter, but when it wasn't jouncing, it slid pitifully from one side to the other, even back when she took her foot from the gas to better weather the ruts. She wished she'd had the foresight to rent a Jeep, if not a Sherman tank. It was all she could do to hold the steering wheel steady. It was all she could do to see the road.

Leah was frightened. Darkness was closing in from every angle, leaving her high beams as a beacon to nowhere. When they picked up an expanse of water directly in her path, she slammed on the brakes. The car fishtailed in the mud, then came to a stop, its sudden stillness compensated for by the racing of her pulse.

A little voice inside her screamed, *turn back! Turn*

back! But she couldn't turn. She was hemmed in on both sides by the woods.

She stared at the water before her. Beneath the pelting rain, it undulated as a living thing. But it was only a puddle, she told herself. Victoria would have mentioned a stream, and there was no sign of a bridge, washed out or otherwise.

Cautiously she stepped on the gas. Yard by yard, the car stole forward. She tried not to think about how high the water might be on the hubcaps. She tried not to think about the prospect of brake damage or stalling. She tried not to think about what creatures of the wild might be lurking beneath the rain-swollen depths. She kept as steady a foot on the gas pedal as possible and released a short sigh of relief when she reached high ground once again.

There were other puddles and ruts and thick beds of mud, but then the road widened. Heart pounding, she squinted through the windshield as she pushed on the accelerator. The cabin had to be ahead. *Please, God, let it be ahead.*

All at once, with terrifying abruptness, the road seemed to disappear. She'd barely had time to jerk her foot to the brake, when the car careened over a rise and began a downward slide. After a harrowing aeon, it came to rest in a deep pocket of sludge.

Shaking all over, Leah closed her eyes for a minute. She took one tremulous breath, then another, then opened her eyes and looked ahead. What she saw took her breath away completely.

For three weeks she'd been picturing a compact and charming log cabin. A chimney would rise from one side; windows would flank the front door. Nestled in the woods, the cabin would be the epitome of a snug country haven.

Instead it was the epitome of ruin. She blinked, convinced that she was hallucinating. Before her lay the charred remains of what might indeed have once been a snug and charming cabin. Now only the chimney was standing.

"Oh, Lord," she wailed, her cry nearly drowned out by the thunder of rain on the roof of the car, "what *happened?*"

Unfortunately what had happened was obvious. There had been a fire. But when? And why hadn't Victoria been notified?

The moan that followed bore equal parts disappointment, fatigue and anxiety. In the confines of the car it had such an eerie edge that Leah knew she had to get back to civilization and fast. At that moment even the thought of spending the night in a fleabag motel held appeal.

She stepped on the gas and the front wheels spun. She shifted into reverse and hit the gas again, but the car didn't budge. Into drive…into reverse…she repeated the cycle a dozen times, uselessly. Not only was she not getting back to civilization she wasn't getting *anywhere,* at least, not in the Golf.

Dropping her head to the steering wheel, she took several shuddering breaths. Leah Gates didn't panic. She hadn't done so when her parents had died. She hadn't done so when her babies had died. She hadn't done so when her husband had pronounced her unfit as a wife and left her.

What she had done in each of those situations was cry until her grief was spent, then pick herself up and restructure her dreams. In essence, that was what she had to do now. There wasn't time to give vent to tears, but a definite restructuring of plans was in order.

She couldn't spend the night in the car. She couldn't get back to town. Help wasn't about to come to her, so...

Fishing the paper with the typed directions from her purse, she turned on the overhead light and read at the bottom of the page the lines that she'd merely skimmed before. True, she'd promised Victoria that she'd deliver the letter to the trapper, Garrick Rodenhiser, but she'd assumed she'd do it at her leisure. Certainly not in the dark of night—or in the midst of a storm.

But seeking out the trapper seemed her only hope of rescue. It was pouring and very dark. She had neither flashlight, umbrella nor rain poncho handy. She'd just have to make a dash for it. Hadn't she done the same often enough in New York when a sudden downpour soaked the streets?

Diligently she reread the directions to the trapper's cabin. Peering through the windshield, she located the break in the woods behind and to the left of the chimney. Without dwelling on the darkness ahead, she tucked the paper back in her purse, dropped the purse to the floor, turned off the lights, then the engine. After pocketing the keys, she took a deep breath, swung open the door and stepped out into the rain.

Her feet promptly sank six inches into mud. Dumbly she stared down at where her ankles should have been. Equally as dumbly she tugged at one foot, which emerged minus its shoe. She stuck her foot back into the mud, rooted around until she'd located the shoe and squished her foot inside, then drew the whole thing up toe first.

After tottering for a second, she lunged onto what she hoped was firmer ground. It was, though this time her other foot came up shoeless. Legs wide apart, she repeated the procedure of retrieving her shoe, then scrambled ahead.

She didn't think about the fact that the comfortable leather flats she'd loved were no doubt ruined. She didn't think about her stockings or her pants or, for that matter, the rest of her clothes, which were already drenched. And assuming that it would be a quick trip to the trapper's cabin, then a quick one back with help, she didn't think once about locking the car. As quickly as she could she ran around the ruins of Victoria's cabin and plunged on into the woods.

An old logging trail, Victoria had called it. Leah could believe that. No car could have fit through, for subsequent years of woodland growth had narrowed it greatly. But it was visible, and for that she was grateful.

It was also wet, and in places nearly as muddy as what she'd so precipitously stepped into from her car. As hastily as she could, she slogged through, only to find her feet mired again a few steps later.

As the minutes passed, she found it harder to will away the discomfort she felt. It occurred to her on a slightly hysterical note that dashing across Manhattan in the rain had never been like this. She was cold and wet. Her clothes clung to her body, providing little if any protection. Her hair was soaked; her bangs dripped into her eyes behind glasses whose lenses were streaked. Tension and the effort of wading through mud made her entire body ache.

Worse, there was no sign of a cabin ahead, or of anything else remotely human. For the first time since her car had become stuck she realized exactly how alone and vulnerable she was. Garrick Rodenhiser was a trapper, which meant that there were animals about. The thought that they might hunt humans in the rain sent shivers through her limbs, over and above those caused by the cold night air. Then she slipped in the mud and lost her balance, falling to the ground with a sharp cry. Sheer terror had her on her feet in an instant, and she whimpered as she struggled on.

Several more times Leah lost a shoe and would have left it if the thought of walking in her sheer-stockinged feet hadn't been far worse than the slimness of the once fine leather. Twice more she fell, crying out in pain the second time when her thigh connected with something sharp. Not caring to consider what it might have been, she limped on. Hopping, sliding, scrambling for a foothold at times, she grew colder, wetter and muddier.

At one point pure exhaustion brought her to a standstill. Her arms and legs were stiff; her insides trembled; her breath came in short, sharp gasps. She had to go on, she told herself, but it was another minute before her limbs would listen. And then it was only because the pain of movement was preferable to the psychological agony of inaction.

When she heard sounds beyond the rain, her panic grew. Glancing blindly behind her, she ricocheted off a tree and spun around, barely saving herself from yet another fall. She was sure she was crying, because she'd never been so frightened in her life, but she couldn't distinguish tears from raindrops.

A world of doubts crowded in on her. How much farther could she push her protesting limbs? How could she be sure that the trapper's cabin still existed? What if Garrick Rodenhiser simply wasn't there? *What would she do then?*

Nearing the point of despair, Leah didn't see the cabin until she was practically on top of it. She stumbled and fell, but on a path of flat stones this time. Shoving up her glasses with the back of one cold, stiff hand, she peered through the rain at the dark structure before her. After a frantic few seconds' search, she spotted the sliver of light that escaped through the shutters. It was the sweetest sight she'd ever seen.

Pushing herself upright, she staggered the final distance and all but crawled up the few short steps to the cabin's door. Beneath the overhang of the porch she was out of the rain, but her teeth were chattering, and her legs abruptly refused to hold her any longer. Sliding down on her bottom close by the door, she mustered the last of her strength to bang her elbow against the wood. Then she wrapped her arms around her middle and tried to hold herself together.

When a minute passed and nothing happened, her misery grew. The cold air of night gusted past her, chilling her wet clothing even more. She tapped more feebly on the wood, but it must have done the trick, for within seconds the door opened. Weakly she raised her eyes. Through wet glasses she could make out a huge form silhouetted in the doorway. Behind it was sanctuary.

"I…" she began, "I…"

The mighty figure didn't move.

"I am…I need…" Her voice was thready, severely impeded by the chill that had reduced her to a shivering mass.

Slowly, cautiously, the giant lowered itself to its haunches. Leah knew it was human. It moved like a human. It had hands like a human. She could only pray that it had the heart of a human.

"Victoria sent me," she whispered. "I'm so cold."

2

Garrick Rodenhiser would have laughed had the huddled figure before him been less pathetic. Victoria wouldn't have sent him a woman; she knew that he valued his privacy too much. And she respected that, which was one of the reasons they'd become friends.

But the figure on his doorstep was indeed pathetic. She was soaking wet, covered with mud and, from the way she was quaking, looked to be chilled to the bone. Of course, the quaking could be from fear, he mused, and if she was handing him a line, she had due cause for fear.

Still, he wasn't an ogre. Regardless of what had brought her here, he couldn't close his door and leave her to the storm.

"Come inside," he said as he closed a hand around her upper arm and started to help her up.

She tried to pull away, whispering a frantic, "I'm filthy!"

The tightening of his fingers was his only response. Leah didn't protest further. Her legs were stiff and sore; she wasn't sure she'd have made it up on her own. His hand fell away, though, the instant she was standing, and he stood back for her to precede him into the cabin.

She took three steps into the warmth, then stopped. Behind her the door closed. Before her the fire blazed. Beneath her was a rapidly spreading puddle of mud.

Removing her glasses, she started to wipe them on her jacket, only to realize after several swipes that it wouldn't help. Glasses dangling, she looked helplessly around.

"Not exactly dressed for the weather, are you?" the trapper asked.

His voice was deep, faintly gravelly. Leah's eyes shot to his face. Though his features were fuzzy, his immense size was not. It had been one thing for him to tower over her when she'd been collapsed on the porch; now she was standing, all five-seven of her. He had to be close to six-four, and was strapping to boot. She wondered if she should fear him.

"Are you Garrick Rodenhiser?" Her voice sounded odd. It was hoarse and as shaky as the rest of her.

He nodded.

She noted that he was dressed darkly and that he was bearded, but if he was who he said, then he was a friend of Victoria's, and she was safe.

"I need help," she croaked, forcing the words out with great effort. "My car got stuck in the mud—"

"You need a shower," Garrick interrupted. He strode to the far side of the room—the large and only room of the cabin—where he opened a closet and drew out several clean towels. Though he didn't know who his guest was, she was not only trembling like a leaf, she was also making a mess on his floor. The sooner she was clean and warm, the sooner she could explain her presence.

Flipping on the bathroom light, he tossed the towels

onto the counter by the sink, then gestured for Leah to come. When she didn't move, he gestured again. "There's plenty of hot water. And soap and shampoo."

Leah looked down at her clothes. They were nearly unrecognizable as those she'd put on that morning. "It wasn't like this in the movie," she cried weakly.

Garrick stiffened, wondering if he was being set up. "Excuse me?"

"*Romancing the Stone*. They went through rain and mud, but their clothes came out looking clean."

He hadn't seen a movie in four years, and whether or not her remark was innocent remained to be seen. "You'd better take them off."

"But I don't have any others." Her body shook; her teeth clicked together between words. "They're in my car."

Garrick set off for the side of the room, where a huge bed shared the wall with a low dresser. He opened one drawer after another, finally returning to toss a pile of neatly folded clothes into the bathroom by the towels.

This time when he gestured, Leah moved. Her gait was stilted, though, and before she'd reached the bathroom, she was stopped by a raspy inquiry.

"What happened to your leg?"

She shot a glance at her thigh and swallowed hard. Not even the coating of mud on her pants could hide the fact that they were torn and she was bleeding. "I fell."

"What did you hit?"

"Something sharp." Rooted to the spot by curiosity as much as fatigue, she watched Garrick head for the part of the room that served as a kitchen, open a cabinet and set a large first-aid kit on the counter. He rummaged through and came up with a bottle of disinfectant and bandaging material, which he then added to the gathering pile in the bathroom.

"Take your shower," he instructed. "I'll make coffee."

"Brandy, I need brandy," she blurted out.

"Sorry. No brandy."

"Whiskey?" she asked more meekly. Didn't all woodsmen drink, preferably the potent, homemade stuff?

"Sorry."

"Anything?" she whispered.

Garrick shook his head. He almost wished he did have something strong. Despite the warmth of the cabin, the woman before him continued to tremble. If she'd trekked through the forest for any distance—and from the look of her she had—she was probably feeling the aftereffects of shock. But he didn't have anything remotely alcoholic to drink. He hadn't so much as looked at a bottle since he'd left California.

"Then hot coffee would...be lovely." She tried to smile, but her face wouldn't work. Nor were her legs eager to function in any trained manner. They protested when she forced them to carry her to the bathroom. She was feeling achier by the minute.

With the tip of one grimy finger, she closed the bathroom door. What she really wanted was a bath, but she quickly saw that there wasn't a tub. The bathroom was large, though, surprisingly modern, bright, clean and well equipped.

"There's a heat lamp," Garrick called from the other side of the door.

She found the switch and turned it on, determinedly avoiding the mirror in the process. Setting her glasses by the sink, she opened the door of the oversize shower stall and turned on the water. The minute it was hot, she stepped in, clothes and all.

It was heaven, sheer heaven. Hot water rained down on her head, spilling over the rest of her in a cascade of instant warmth. She didn't know how long she stood there without moving, nor did she care. Garrick had offered plenty of hot water, and despite the fact that she'd never been one to be selfish or greedy, she planned to take advantage of every drop. These were extenuating circumstances, she reasoned. After the ordeal she'd been through, her body deserved a little pampering.

Moreover, standing under the shower was as much of a limbo as the highway driving had been earlier. She knew that once she emerged, she was going to have to face a future that was as mucked up as her clothes. She wasn't looking forward to it.

Gradually the numbness in her hands and feet wore off. Slowly, and with distaste, she began to strip off her things. When every last item lay in a pile in a corner of the stall, she went to work with soap and shampoo, lathering, rinsing, lathering, rinsing, continuing the process far longer than was necessary, almost obsessive in her need to rid herself of the mud that was synonymous with terror.

By the time she turned off the water, the ache in her limbs had given way to a pervasive tiredness. More than anything at that moment she craved a soft chair, if not a sofa or, better yet, a bed. But there was work to be done first. Emerging from the shower, she wrapped one towel around her hair, then began to dry herself with another. When she inadvertently ran the towel over her thigh, she gasped. Fumbling for her glasses, she rinsed and dried them, then shakily fit them onto her nose.

She almost wished she hadn't. Her outer thigh bore a deep, three-inch gash that was ugly enough to make her stomach turn. Straightening, she closed her eyes, pressed a hand to her middle and took several deep breaths. Then, postponing another look for as long as possible, she reached for the clothes Garrick had left.

Beggars couldn't be choosers, which was why she thought no evil of the gray thermal top she pulled on and the green flannel shirt she layered over it. The thermal top hit her upper thigh; the shirt was even longer. The warmth of both was welcome.

Tucking the tails beneath her, she lowered herself to the closed commode. Working quickly, lest she lose her nerve, she opened the bottle of disinfectant, poured a liberal amount on a corner of the towel and pressed it firmly to the gash.

White-hot pain shot through her leg. Crying aloud, she tore the towel away. At the same time, her other hand went boneless, releasing its grip on the bottle, which fell to the floor and shattered.

Garrick, who'd been standing pensively before the fire, jerked up his head when he heard her cry. Within seconds he'd crossed the floor and burst into the bathroom.

Leah's hands were fisted on her knees, and she was rocking back and forth, waiting for the stinging in her leg to subside. Her gaze flew to his. "I didn't think it would hurt so much," she whispered.

His grip tightened on the doorknob, and for a split second he considered retreating. It had been more than four years since he'd seen legs like those—long and slender, living silk the color of cream. His eyes were riveted to them, while his heart yawed. He told himself to turn and run—until he caught sight of the red gouge marring that silk and knew he wasn't going anywhere.

Squatting before her, he took the towel from where it lay across her lap and dabbed at the area around the cut. The color of the antiseptic was distinct on the corner of the towel she'd used. He reversed the terry cloth and flicked her a glance.

"Hold on."

With a gentle dabbing motion, he applied whatever disinfectant was left on the towel to her cut. She sucked in her breath and splayed one hand tightly over the top of her thigh to hold it still. Even then her leg was shaking badly by the time Garrick reached for the bandages.

"I can do it," she breathed. Beads of sweat had broken out on her nose, causing her glasses to slip. Her fingers trembled when she shoved them up, but she was feeling foolish about the broken bottle and needed desperately to show her grit.

She might as well not have spoken. Garrick proceeded to cover the wound with a large piece of gauze and strap it in place with adhesive tape. When that was done, he carefully collected the largest pieces of broken glass and set them on the counter.

He looked at her then, eyes skimming her pale features before coming to rest on her temple. Taking a fresh piece of gauze, he dipped it into the small amount of liquid left in the bottom quarter of the bottle and, with the same gentle dabbing, disinfected the cluster of scratches he'd found.

Leah hadn't been aware of their existence. She vaguely recalled reeling off a tree, but surface scratches had been the least of her worries when the rest of her had been so cold and sore. Even now the scratches were quickly forgotten, because Garrick had turned his attention to her hand that had remained in a fist throughout the procedure. She held her breath when he reached for it.

Without asking himself why or to what end, he slowly and carefully unclenched her fingers, then stared at the purple crescents her short nails had left on her palm. They were a testament to the kind of self-control he admired; even when he brushed his thumb across them, willing them away, they remained. Cradling her hand in his far larger one, he raised his eyes to hers.

She wasn't prepared for their luminous force. They penetrated her, warmed her, frightened her in ways she didn't understand. Hazel depths spoke of loneliness; silver flecks spoke of need. They reached out and enveloped her, demanding nothing, demanding everything.

It was an incredible moment.

Of all the new experiences she'd had that day, this was the most stunning. For Garrick Rodenhiser wasn't the grizzled old trapper she'd assumed she'd find in a rustic cabin in the woods. He was a man in his prime, and the only scents emanating from him had to do with wood smoke and maleness.

At that most improbable and unexpected time, she was drawn to him.

Unable to cope with the idea of being drawn to anyone, least of all a total stranger, she looked away. But
she wasn't the only one stunned by the brief visual in-
terlude. Garrick, too, was pricked by new and unbidden
emotions.

Abruptly releasing her hand, he stood. "Don't touch
the glass," he ordered gruffly. "I'll take care of it when
you're done." Turning on his heel, he left the bathroom
and strode back to the hearth. He was still there, bent
over the mantel with his forearms on the rough wood
and his forehead on his arms, when he heard the sound
of the bathroom door opening sometime later.

With measured movements he straightened and
turned, fully prepared to commence his inquisition.
This woman, whoever she was, was trespassing on his
turf. He didn't like uninvited visitors. He didn't like
anything remotely resembling a threat to his peace.

He hadn't counted on what he'd see, much less what
he'd feel when he saw it. If he'd thought he'd gained
control of his senses during those few minutes alone,
he'd been mistaken. Now, looking at this woman about
whom he knew absolutely nothing, he was shaken by
the same desire that had shocked his system earlier.

Strangely, if that desire had been physical, he'd have
felt less threatened. Hormonal needs were understand-
able, acceptable, easily slaked.

But what he felt went beyond the physical. It had first
sparked when he'd barged into the bathroom and seen
legs that were feminine, ivory, sleek and exposed. There
had been nothing seductive about the way they'd trembled, but he'd been disturbed anyway. He had thought
of a doe he'd encountered in the woods; the animal had

stared at him, motionless save for the faint tremor in her hind legs that betrayed an elemental fear. He'd been frustrated then, unable to assure the doe that he'd never harm her. He was frustrated now because the woman seemed equally as defenseless, and while he might have assured her, he wasn't able to form the words.

The desire he felt had grown during his ministrations, when his fingers had brushed her thigh and found it to be warmed from the shower and smooth, so smooth. Very definitely human and alive. A member of his own species. At that moment, he'd felt an instinctive need for assurance from her that he was every bit as human and alive.

When he'd cupped her hand in his, he'd felt the oddest urge to guard her well. Fragility, the need for protection, a primal plea for closeness…he'd been unable to deny the feelings, though they shocked him.

And when he'd searched her eyes, he'd found them as startled as his own must have been.

He wasn't sure if he believed she was genuine; he'd known too many quality actors in his day to take anything at face value. What he couldn't ignore, though, were his own feelings, for they said something about himself that he didn't want to know.

Those feelings hit him full force as he stared at her. It wasn't that she was beautiful. Her black hair, clean now and unturbaned, was damp and straight, falling just shy of her collarbone, save for the bangs that covered her brow. Her features were average, her face dominated by the owl-eyed glasses that perched on her nose. No, she wasn't beautiful, and certainly not sexy wearing his shirt and long johns. But her pallor did something to him, as did the slight forward curve of her shoulders as she wrapped her arms around her waist.

She was the image of vulnerability, and watching her, he felt vulnerable himself. He wanted to hold her, that was all, just to hold her. He couldn't understand it, didn't want to admit it, but it was so.

"I'm not sure what to do with my clothes," she said. Her eyes registered bewilderment, though her voice was calm. "I rinsed them out as best I could. Is there somewhere I can hang them to dry?"

Garrick was grateful for the mundaneness of the question, which allowed him to sidestep those deeper thoughts. "You'd better put them through a real wash first. Over there." He inclined his head toward the kitchen area.

Through clean, dry glasses, Leah saw what she hadn't been physically or emotionally capable of seeing earlier. A washer-dryer combo stood beyond the sink, not far from a dishwasher and a microwave oven. Modern kitchen, modern bathroom—Garrick Rodenhiser, it seemed, roughed it only to a point.

Ducking back into the bathroom, she retrieved her clothes and put them into the washer with a generous amount of detergent. Once the machine was running, she eyed the coffeemaker and its fresh, steaming pot.

"Help yourself," Garrick said. Resuming his silence, he watched her open one cabinet after another until she'd found a mug.

"Will you have some?" she asked without turning.

"No."

Her hand trembled as she poured the coffee, and even the small movement had repercussions in the tension-weary muscles of her shoulders. Cup in hand, she padded barefoot across the floor to peer through the small opening between the shutters that served as drapes. She couldn't see much of anything, but the steady beat of rain on the roof told her what she wanted to know.

Straightening, she turned to face Garrick. "Is there any chance of getting to my car tonight?"

"No."

His single word was a confirmation of what she'd already suspected. There seemed no point in railing against what neither of them could change. "Do you mind if I sit by your fire?"

He stepped aside in silent invitation.

The wide oak planks were warm under her bare feet as she crossed to the hearth. Lowering herself to the small rag rug with more fatigue than finesse, she tucked her legs under her, pressed her arms to her sides and cupped the coffee with both hands.

The flames danced low and gently, and would have been soothing had she been capable of being soothed. But sitting before them, relatively warm and safe for the first time in hours, she saw all too clearly what she faced tonight. She was here for the night; she knew that much. The storm continued. Her car wouldn't move. She was going nowhere until morning. But what then?

Even once her car was freed, she had nowhere to go. Victoria's cabin was gone, and with it the plans she'd spent the past three weeks making. It had all seemed so simple; now nothing was simple. She could look around for another country cabin to rent, but she didn't know where to begin. She could take a room at an inn, but her supply of money was far from endless. She could return to New York, but something about that smacked of defeat—or so she told herself when she found no other excuse for her hesitancy to take that particular option.

If she'd felt unsettled during the drive north, now she felt thoroughly disoriented. Not even at her lowest points in the past had she been without a home.

Behind her, the sofa springs creaked. Garrick. With her glasses on, she'd seen far more than details of the cabin. She'd also seen that Garrick Rodenhiser was extraordinarily handsome. The bulk that had originally impressed her was concentrated in his upper body, in the well-developed shoulders and back defined by a thick black turtleneck. Dark gray corduroys molded a lean pair of hips and long, powerful legs. He was bearded, yes, but twenty-twenty vision revealed that beard to be closely trimmed. And though his hair was on the long side, it, too, was far from unruly and was an attractive dark blond shot through with silver.

His nose was straight, his lips thin and masculine. His skin was stretched over high cheekbones, but his eyes were what held the true force of his being. Silvery hazel, they were alive with questions unasked and thoughts unspoken.

Had Leah been a gambler, she'd have bet that Garrick was a transplant. He simply didn't fit the image of a trapper. There were the amenities in the cabin, for one thing, which spoke of a certain sophistication. There was also his speech; though his words were few and far between, his enunciation was cultured. And his eyes—those eyes—held a worldly look, realistic, cynical, simultaneously knowing and inquisitive.

She wondered where he'd come from and what had brought him here. She wondered what he thought of her arrival and of the fact that she'd be spending the night. She wondered what kind of a man he was where women were concerned, and whether the need she'd sensed in him went as deep as, in that fleeting moment in the bathroom, it had seemed.

Garrick was wondering similar things. In his forty years, he'd had more women than he cared to count. From the age of fourteen he'd been aware of himself as a man. Increasingly his ego and his groin had been rivals in his search for and conquest of woman. As the years had passed, quantity had countermanded quality; he'd laid anything feminine, indiscriminately and often with little care. He'd used and been used, and the sexual skill in which he'd once taken pride had been reduced to a physical act that was shallow and hurtful. It had reflected the rest of his life too well.

All that had ended four years ago. When he'd first come to New Hampshire, he'd stayed celibate. He hadn't yearned, hadn't wanted. He'd lived within well-defined walls, unsure of himself, distrusting his emotions and motivations. During those early months his sole goal had been to forge out an existence as a human being.

Gradually, the day-to-day course of his life had fallen into place. He'd had the occasional woman since then, though not out of any gut-wrenching desire as much as the simple need to assure himself that he was male and normal. Rarely had he seen the same woman twice. Never had he brought one to his home.

But one was here now. He hadn't asked for her. In

fact, he wanted her gone as soon as possible. Yet even as he studied her, as he watched her stare into the fire, take an occasional sip of coffee, flex her arms around herself protectively, he felt an intense need for human contact.

He wondered if the need was indicative of a new stage in his redevelopment, if he'd reached the point of being comfortable with himself and was now ready to share himself with others.

To share. To *learn* to share. He'd always been self-centered, and to an extent, the life he'd built here reinforced that. He did what he wanted when he wanted. He wasn't sure if he was capable of changing that, or if he wanted to change it. He wasn't sure if he was ready to venture into something new.

Still, there was the small voice of need that cried out when he looked at her....

"What's your name?"

His voice came so unexpectedly that Leah jumped. Her head shot around, eyes wide as they met his. "Leah Gates."

"You're a friend of Victoria's?"

"Yes."

He shifted his gaze to the flames. Only when she had absorbed the dismissal and turned back to the fire herself did he look at her again.

Leah Gates. A friend of Victoria's. His mind conjured up several possibilities, none of which was entirely reassuring. She could indeed be a friend of Victoria's, an acquaintance who'd somehow learned of his existence and had decided, for whatever her reasons, to seek him out. On the other hand she could be lying outright, using Victoria's name to get the story that no one else had been able to get. Or she could be telling the truth, which left the monumental question of why Victoria would have sent her to him.

Only two facts were clear. The first was that he was stuck with her; she wasn't going anywhere for a while. The second was that she'd been through a minor ordeal getting here and that, even as she sat before the fire, she'd begun to tremble again.

Pushing himself from the sofa, he went for the spare quilt that lay neatly folded on the end of the bed. He shook it out as he returned to the fire, then draped it lightly over her shoulders. She sent him a brief but silent word of thanks before tugging it closely around her.

This time when he sank onto the sofa it was with a vague sense of satisfaction. He ignored it at first, but it lingered, and at length he deigned to consider it. He'd never been one to give. His life—that life—had been ruled by selfishness and egotism. That as small a gesture as offering a quilt should please him was interesting…encouraging…puzzling.

As the evening passed, the only sounds in the cabin were the crackle of the fire and the echo of the rain. From time to time Garrick added another log to the grate, and after a bit, Leah curled onto her side beneath the quilt. He knew the very moment she fell asleep, for the fingers that clutched the quilt so tightly relaxed and her breathing grew steady.

Watching her sleep, he felt it again, the need to hold and be held, the need to protect. His fertile mind created a scenario in which Leah was a lost soul with no ties to the past, no plans for the future, no need beyond that of a little human warmth. It was a dream, of course, but it reflected what he hadn't glimpsed about himself until tonight. He didn't think he liked it, because it meant that something was lacking in the life he'd so painstakingly shaped for himself, but it was there, and it had a sudden and odd kind of power.

Rising silently from the sofa this time, he got down on his haunches beside her. Her face was half-hidden, so he eased the quilt down to her chin, studying features lit only by the dying embers in the hearth. She looked totally guileless; he wished he could believe that she was.

Unable to help himself, he touched the back of his fingers to her cheek. Her skin was soft and unblemished, warmed by the fire, faintly flushed. Dry now, her hair was thick. The bangs that covered her brow made her features look all the more delicate. She wasn't beautiful or sexy, but he had to give her pretty. If only he could give her innocent.

It wouldn't hurt to pretend for one night, would it?

Careful not to disturb her, he gently slid his arms beneath her and, quilt and all, carried her to his bed. When she was safely tucked into one side, he crossed to the other, stripped down to his underwear and stretched out beneath the sheets.

Lying flat on his back, he tipped his head her way. The black gloss of her hair was all he could see above the quilt, but the series of lumps beneath it suggested far more. She wasn't curvaceous. Her drenched clothes had clung to a slender body. And she wasn't heavy. He knew; he'd carried her. Still, even when she'd been covered with mud and soaked, he'd known she was a woman.

Eyes rising to the darkened rafters, he shifted once, paused, then shifted again. With each shift, he inched closer to her. He couldn't feel her warmth, couldn't smell her scent. Multiple layers of bedclothes, plus a safe twelve inches of space prevented that. But he knew she was there, and in the dark, where no one could see or know, he smiled.

Leah awoke the next morning to the smell of fresh coffee and the sizzle of bacon. She was frowning even before she'd opened her eyes, because she didn't understand who would be in her apartment, much less making breakfast. Then the events of the day before returned to her, and her eyes flew open. Last she remembered she'd been lying in front of the fire. Now she was in a bed. But there was only one bed in Garrick's cabin.

Garrick. Her head spun around and she saw a blurred form before the stove. Moments later, with her glasses firmly in place, she confirmed the identity of that form.

It took her a minute to free herself from the cocoon of quilts and another minute to push herself up and drop her feet to the floor. In the process she was scolded by every sore muscle in her body. Gritting back a moan, she rose from the bed and limped into the bathroom.

By the time she'd washed up and combed her hair, she was contemplating sneaking back to bed. She ached all over, she looked like hell, and from the sounds of it, the rain hadn't let up. Going out in the storm, even in daylight, was a dismal thought.

But she couldn't sneak back to bed because the bed wasn't hers. And he'd seen her get up. And she had decisions to make.

Garrick had just set two plates of food on the small table, when she hesitantly approached. His keen glance took in her pale skin and the gingerliness of her movements. "Sit," he commanded, refusing to be touched. He'd had his one night of pretending and resented the fact that it had left him wanting. Now morning had come, and he needed some answers.

Leah sat—and proceeded, with no encouragement at all, to consume an indeterminate number of scrambled eggs, four rashers of bacon, two corn muffins, a large glass of orange juice and a cup of coffee. She was working on a second cup, when she realized what she'd done. Peering sheepishly over the rim of the cup, she murmured, "Sorry about that. I guess I was hungry."

"No dinner last night?"

"No dinner." It must have been close to eight o'clock when she'd finally stumbled to his door. Not once had she thought of food, even when she'd passed the stove en route to the washing machine. With an intake of breath at the memory, she started to get up. "I left my clothes in the washer—"

"They're dry." He'd switched them into the dryer after she'd fallen asleep. "All except the sweater. I hung it up. Don't think it should have been washed, being cashmere."

He'd drawled the last with a hint of sarcasm, but Leah was feeling too self-conscious to catch it. She hadn't had anyone tend to her in years. That Garrick should be doing it—a total stranger handling her clothes, her underthings—was disturbing. Even worse, he'd carried her to his bed, and she'd slept there with him. Granted, she'd been oblivious to it all, but in the light of day she was far from oblivious to the air of potent masculinity he projected. He looked unbelievably rugged, yet unconscionably civilized. Fresh from the shower, his hair was damp. In a hunter green turtleneck and tan cords that matched the color of his hair and beard, he was gorgeous.

"It was probably ruined long before I put it in the washer," she murmured breathily, then darted an awkward glance toward the window. "How long do you think the rain will last?"

"Days."

She caught his gaze and forced a laugh. "Thanks." When she saw no sign of a returning smile, her own faded. "You're serious, aren't you." It wasn't a question.

"Very."

"But I need my car."

"Where is it?"

"At Victoria's cabin."

"Why?"

"Why do I need it?" She'd have thought that would be obvious.

"Why is it at Victoria's?"

In a rush, Leah remembered how little she and Garrick had spoken the night before. "Because she was renting the cabin to me, only when I got there, I saw that it was nothing but—" She didn't finish, because Garrick was eyeing her challengingly. That, combined with the way he was sitting—leaning far back in his chair with one hand on his thigh and the other toying with his mug—evoked an illusion of menace. At least, she hoped it was only an illusion.

"You said that Victoria sent you to me," he reminded her tightly.

"That's right."

"In what context?"

The nervousness Leah was feeling caused her words to tumble out with uncharacteristic speed. "She said that if I had a problem, you'd be able to help. And I have a problem. The cabin's burned down, my car is stuck in the mud, I have to find somewhere to stay because my apartment's gone—"

"Victoria sent you to stay in the cabin," he stated, seeming to weigh the words.

Leah didn't like his tone. "Is there a problem with that?"

"Yes."

"What is it?"

He didn't blink an eye. "Victoria's cabin burned three months ago."

For a minute she said nothing. Then she asked very quietly, "What?"

"The cabin burned three months ago."

"That can't be."

"It is."

If it had been three days ago, Leah might have understood. With a stretch of the imagination, she might even have believed three weeks. After all, no one was living at the cabin. To her knowledge Garrick wasn't its caretaker. But three *months?* Surely someone would have been by during that time. "You're telling me that the cabin burned three months ago and that Victoria wasn't told?"

"I'm telling you that the cabin burned three months ago."

"Why wasn't Victoria *told?*" Leah demanded impatiently.

"She was."

Her anger rose. "I don't believe you."

Garrick was staring at her straight and hard. "I called her myself, then gave the insurance people a tour."

"Call her now. We'll see what she knows."

"I don't have a phone."

Given the other modern amenities in the cabin, Leah couldn't believe there was no phone. She looked around a little frantically for an instrument that would connect her with the outside world but saw nothing remotely resembling one. Then she remembered Victoria saying that she didn't have a phone at her cabin, either.

Why would she have said that, if she'd known that she didn't have a *cabin?*

"She didn't know about the fire," Leah insisted.

"She did."

"You're lying."

"I don't lie."

"You have to be lying," she declared, but her voice had risen in pitch. "Because if you're not, the implication is that Victoria sent me up here knowing full well that I wouldn't be able to stay. And that's preposterous."

The coffee cup began to shake in her hand. She set it on the table and wrapped her arms around her waist in a gesture Garrick had seen her make before. It suggested distress, but whether that distress was legitimate remained to be seen.

He said nothing, simply stared at the confusion that clouded her eyes.

"She wouldn't do that," Leah whispered pleadingly, wanting, needing to believe it. "For three weeks she's been listening to me—helping me—make plans. I stored all my furniture, notified the electric company, the phone company, my friends. Victoria personally gave me a set of typed directions and sat by while I read them. She wouldn't have gone to the effort—or let me go to the effort—if she'd known the cabin was useless."

Garrick, too, was finding it hard to believe, but it was Leah's story rather than Victoria's alleged behavior that evoked his skepticism. Yes, Leah looked confused, but perhaps that was part of the act. If she'd set out to find him, she'd done it. She was in his cabin, wearing his clothing, eating his food, drinking his coffee. She'd even spent the night in his bed, albeit innocently. If she wanted a scoop on Greg Reynolds, she'd positioned herself well.

"Who are you?" he asked.

Her head shot up. "I told you. Leah Gates."

"Where are you from?"

"New York."

"I don't suppose you happen to work for a newspaper," he commented, fully expecting an immediate denial. He was momentarily surprised when her eyes lit up.

"How did you know?"

He grunted.

She didn't know what to make of that, any more than she knew what to make of the fact that his lips were set tautly, almost angrily, within the confines of his beard.

"Have you seen my name?" she asked. If he was a crossword addict, as were so many of her fans, her name would have rung a bell.

"I don't read papers."

"Then you've seen one of my books?"

"You write books, too?" he barked.

His question and its tone had her thoroughly perplexed. "I compose crossword puzzles. They appear in a small weekly paper, but I've had several full books of puzzles published."

Crossword puzzles? A likely story. Still, if she was a reporter, she couldn't be an actress—which didn't explain why her words sounded so sincere. "Why were you moving up here?" he asked in a more tempered tone of voice.

"I lost my apartment and I wasn't sure where to go, so Victoria suggested I rent her cabin for a while until I decided." She dropped a frowning gaze to the table as she mumbled, "It seemed like a good idea at the time."

Garrick said nothing.

In the ensuing silence, Leah reran the past few minutes of conversation in her mind. Then, slowly, her eyes rose. "You don't believe what I'm saying. Why not?"

He hadn't expected such forthrightness, and when she looked at him that way, all honesty and vulnerability, he was the one confused. He couldn't tell her the truth. After staunchly guarding his identity for four years, he wasn't about to blow it by making an accusation that revealed all.

So he lifted one shoulder in a negligent shrug. "It's not often that a woman chooses to live up here alone. I take it you are alone."

She hesitated before offering a tentative, "Yes."

Good Lord, could she have a photographer stashed somewhere about? "*Are* you?"

"Yes!"

"Then why the pause?"

Leah's eyes flashed. She wasn't used to having her integrity questioned. "When you've spent your entire life in New York, you think twice about giving a man certain information. It's instinct."

"It's distrust."

"Then we're even!"

"But you did answer me."

"Victoria said you were a friend. I trust her judgment. She even gave me a letter to deliver to you."

He extended one large hand, palm up, in invitation. The smug twist of his lips only heightened her defensiveness.

"If it were on me, you'd have had it by now," she cried. "It's in my car, along with my purse and everything else I own in the world."

"Except for your furniture," he remarked, dropping his hand back to his thigh.

She made a little sound of defeat. "Yes."

"And you can't get to your car. You may not be able to get there for days. You're stuck here with me."

Leah shook her head, willing away that prospect. It wasn't that Garrick was repulsive; indeed, the opposite was true. But while there was a side to him that was gentle and considerate, there was another more cynical side, and that frightened her. "I'll get to my car later."

"Unless the rain lets up, you're not going anywhere."

"I have to get to my car."

"How?"

"The same way I got here. If you won't drive me, I'll walk."

"It's not that I *won't* drive you, Leah," he said, using her name for the first time. "It's that I *can't*. You've arrived up here at the onset of mud season, and during mud season, no one moves! The sturdiest of vehicles is useless. The roads are impassable." Arching a brow, he stroked his bearded jaw with his knuckles. "Tell me. What was it like driving the road to Victoria's cabin last night?"

"Hell."

"And walking from Victoria's to mine?"

The look she sent him was eloquent.

"Well, it'll be worse today and even worse tomorrow. At this time of year, snow melts from the upper mountain and drains down over ground that is already thawing and soggy. When the rain comes, forget it."

But Leah didn't want to. "Maybe if we walk back to the car and I get behind the wheel and you push—"

"I'm neither a bulldozer nor a tow truck, and let me tell you, I'm not even sure one of those would do the trick. I've seen off-road vehicles get stuck on roads far less steep than the ones on this hill."

"It's worth a try."

"It isn't."

"Victoria said you'd help me."

"I am. I'm offering you a place to stay."

"But I can't stay here!"

"You don't have much choice."

"You can't *want* me to stay here!"

"I don't have much choice."

With a helpless little moan, Leah rose from the table and went to stare bleakly out the window. He was right, she supposed. She didn't have much choice. She could go out in the rain and trek back to her car, but if what he said was true—and he'd certainly be in a position to know—she'd simply find herself back on his doorstep, wet, muddy, exhausted and humiliated.

This wasn't at all what she'd had in mind when she'd left New York!

3

The clatter of pans in the sink brought Leah from her self-indulgent funk a short time later. Feeling instantly contrite, she returned to the kitchen. Garrick had already loaded the dishwasher; taking a towel, she began to dry the pans as he washed them.

They worked in silence. When the last skillet had been put away, she folded the towel and placed it neatly on the counter. "I'm sorry," she said quietly. She didn't look at Garrick, who was wiping down the sink. "I must have sounded ungrateful, and I'm not. I appreciate what you're doing." Pausing, she searched for suitably tactful words. "It's just that this isn't quite what I'd planned."

"What had you planned?"

"Sunshine and fresh air. A cabin all to myself. Plenty of time to work and read and walk in the woods. And cook—" She looked up in alarm at the thought. "I have food in the car! It'll spoil if I don't get it refrigerated!"

"It's cold outside."

"Cold enough?"

"Depends on what kind of food you have."

She would have listed off an inventory had there

been any point. But there wasn't, so she simply let out a breath of resignation. He'd made it clear that she couldn't get to her car. Whatever spoiled would spoil.

Tugging the lapels of the flannel shirt more tightly around her, she sent him a pleading glance. "This is the first time I've even thought of living outside New York, and to have things go wrong is upsetting. I still can't understand why Victoria offered me the cabin."

Garrick was beginning to entertain one particularly grating suspicion. Eyes dark, he set the dishrag aside and retreated to the living room. The sofa took his weight with multiple creaks of protest, but the protests in his mind were even louder.

Leah remained where she was for several minutes, waiting for him to speak. He was clearly upset; his brooding slouch was as much a giveaway as the low shelving of his brows. And he had a right to be upset, she told herself. No man who'd chosen to live alone on a secluded mountainside deserved to have that seclusion violated.

Studying him, taking in the power that radiated from even his idle body, she wondered why he'd chosen the life he had. He wasn't an avid conversationalist. But, then, neither was she, yet she'd functioned well in the city. He'd left it—at least, that was what she assumed, though perhaps it was an ingrained snobbishness telling her that the cultured ring to his speech and his fondness for certain luxuries were urban-born. In any case, she couldn't believe that a simple housing problem such as the one she'd faced had sent him into exile. For that matter, he didn't look as though he were in exile at all; he looked as though he were here to stay.

Leah took advantage of his continued distraction to examine the cabin in its entirety. A large, rectangular room with the fireplace and bed on opposite sides, it had a kitchen spread along part of the back wall, leaving space for the bathroom and what looked to be a closet. Large windows flanked the front door. Sandwiched between door, windows, furniture and appliances were bookshelves—a small one here, a larger one there, each and every one brimming with books.

They explained, in part, what Garrick Rodenhiser did with his time. He wasn't reading now, though. He was sitting as he'd been before, staring at the ashes in the hearth. While moments before he'd been brooding, his profile had mellowed to something she couldn't quite define. Loneliness? Sorrow? Confusion?

Or was she simply putting a name to her own feelings?

Unwilling to believe that, despite the clenching of her heart at the sight of Garrick, she looked desperately around for something to do. Her eye fell on the bed, still mussed from the night they'd spent. Crossing the room, she straightened the sheets and quilt, then folded the spare one he'd wrapped around her and set it at the foot of the bed.

What else? She scanned the cabin again, but there was little that needed attention. Everything was neat, clean, organized.

At a loss, she walked quietly to the window. The woods were gray, shrouded in fog, drenched in rain. The bleakness of the scene only emphasized the strange emptiness she felt.

Garrick's deep voice came out of the blue. "What, exactly, is your relationship to Victoria?"

Startled, Leah half turned to find herself the object of his grim scrutiny. "We're friends."

"You've said that. When did you meet?"

"Last year."

"Where?"

"The public library. Victoria was researching the aborigines of New Zealand. We literally bumped into each other."

His expression turned wry, then softened into a reluctant smile. "The aborigines of New Zealand—that does sound like Victoria. Is she going back to school in anthropology?"

"Not exactly," Leah answered, but she had to force herself to think, because his smile—lean lips curving upward between mustache and beard, the flash of even, white teeth—momentarily absorbed her. "She is, uh, she was fascinated by an article she'd read about the Maori, so she decided to visit. She was preparing for the trip when I met her."

"Did she get there?"

"To New Zealand? What do you think?"

Garrick thought yes, and his eyes said as much, but his mind returned quickly to Leah. "Why were you at the library?"

"I often work there—sometimes doing research for puzzles, sometimes just for the change of scenery."

"So you and Victoria became friends. How old are you?"

"Thirty-three."

He pushed out his lips in surprise. "I'd have given you twenty-eight or twenty-nine—" the lips straightened "—but even at thirty-three, there's quite a gap between you."

"But there isn't," Leah returned with quiet vehemence, even wonder. "That's what's so great about Victoria. She's positively…positively amaranthine."

"Amaranthine?"

"Unfading, undying, timeless. Her bio may list her as fifty-three, but she has the body of a forty-year-old, the mind of a thirty-year-old, the enthusiasm of a twenty-year-old and the heart of a child."

The description was one Garrick might have made, though he'd never have been able to express it as well. At the height of his career he'd been a master technician, able to deliver lines from a script with precisely the feeling the director wanted. But no amount of arrogance—and he'd had more than his share—could have made him try to write that script himself.

So Leah did know Victoria, and well. That ruled out one possible lie but left open another. Even knowing that she would compromise her friendship with Victoria, Leah might have taken it upon herself to find and interview the man who'd once been the heartthrob of every woman between the ages of sixteen and sixty-five. Every woman who watched television, that is. Did Leah watch television? Even if she'd come here in total innocence, wouldn't she recognize him?

Shifting his gaze back to the hearth, Garrick lapsed into silence once again. He was recalling how worried he'd been when he'd first arrived in New Hampshire. Each time he'd gone into town for supplies, he'd kept his head down, his eyes averted. Each time he'd waited in dread for telling whispers, tiny squeals, the thrust of pen and paper under his nose.

In fact, he'd looked different from the man who'd graced the television screens of America on a weekly basis for seven years running. His hair was longer, less perfectly styled, and he'd stopped rinsing out the sprinkles of silver that once upon a time he'd been sure would detract from his appeal.

The beard had made a difference, too, but in those early months he'd worried that sharp eyes would see through it to the jaw about which critics had raved. He'd dressed without distinction, wearing the oldest clothes he'd had. Above all, he'd prayed that the mere improbability of a one-time megastar living on a mountainside in the middle of nowhere would shield him from discovery.

With the passing of time—during which he wasn't recognized—he'd gained confidence. He made eye contact. He held his head higher.

Body language. A fascinating thing. He wasn't innocent enough to think that the recognition factor alone had determined the set of his head. No, he'd held his head higher because he felt better about himself. He was learning to live with nature, learning to provide for himself, learning to respect himself as a clean-living human being.

Buoyed by that confidence, he turned to Leah. "You've come to know Victoria well in a year. You must have spent a lot of time with her."

Leah, who'd eyed him steadily during his latest bout of silence, was more prepared for its end this time. "I did."

"Socially?"

"If you're asking whether I went to her parties, the answer is no."

"Are you married?"

"No."

"Have you ever been?" It wasn't crucial to the point of his investigation, but he was curious.

"Yes."

"Divorced?"

She nodded.

"Recently?"

"It's been final for two years."

"Do you date?"

"Do you?"

"I'm asking the questions."

"That's obvious, but I'd like to know why. I'm beginning to feel like I'm on a hot seat."

She sounded hurt. She looked hurt. Garrick surprised himself by feeling remorse, but he was too close to the answer he sought to give up. He did make an effort to soften his tone. "Bear with me. There's a point to all this."

"Mmm. To make me turn tail and run. Believe me, I would if I could. I know that you don't like the idea of a stranger invading your home, but you're a stranger to me, too, and I'm not so much an invader as a refugee, and if you think I like feeling like a refugee, you're nuts…" Her voice faded as her eyes began to skip around the cabin. "Paper and pencil?"

Garrick was nonplussed. "What—"

"If I don't write it down, I'll forget."

"Write what down?"

"The idea—nuts, nutty, nutty as a fruitcake, having bats in one's belfry. Perfect for a theme puzzle." She was moving her hand, simulating a scribble. "Paper?"

Bemused, Garrick cocked his head toward the kitchen. "Second drawer to the left of the sink."

Within seconds, she was jotting down the phrases she'd spoken aloud, adding several others to the list before she'd straightened. Tearing off the sheet, she folded it and tucked it into her breast pocket, returned the pad and pen to the drawer, then sent him a winsome smile. "Where were we?"

Garrick didn't try to fight the warm feeling that settled in his chest. "Do you do that a lot?"

"Write down ideas? Uh-huh."

"You really do make crossword puzzles?"

"You didn't believe me about that, either?"

He moved his head in a way that could have been positive, negative or sheepish. "I've never really thought about people doing it."

"Someone has to."

He considered that for a minute, uttered a quiet, "True," then withdrew into his private world again.

Wondering how long he'd be gone this time, Leah walked softly toward the bookshelf nearest her. Its shelves had a wide array of volumes, mostly works of fiction that had been on bestselling lists in recent years. The books were predominantly hardbacked, their paper sheaths worn where they'd been held. Both facts were revealing. Not only did Garrick read everything he bought, but he bought the latest and most expensive, rather than waiting for cheaper mass market editions.

He wasn't a pauper, that was for sure. Leah wondered where he got the money.

"It must be difficult," came his husky voice. "Finding the right words that will fit together, coming up with witty clues."

It took Leah a minute to realize that he was talking about crossword puzzles. She had to smile. He faded in and out, but the train of his thought ran along a continuous track. "It is a challenge," she admitted.

"I'd never be able to do it."

"That's okay. I'd never be able to lay traps, catch animals and gut them." She'd offered the words in innocence and was appalled at how critical they sounded. Turning to qualify them, she lost out to Garrick's quicker tongue.

"Is that what Victoria told you I do?"

"She said you were a trapper," Leah answered with greater deference, then added meekly, "I'm afraid the elaboration was my own."

His expression was guarded. "What else did Victoria say about me?"

"Only what I told you before—that you were a friend and could be trusted. To be honest, I was expecting someone a little—" she shifted a shoulder "—different."

He raised one eyebrow in question.

"Older. Craggier." Blushing, she looked off across the room. "When Victoria handed me that envelope, I asked her if it was a love letter."

"How do you know it wasn't?" Garrick asked evenly.

Come to think of it, Leah didn't know. She recalled Victoria saying something vague about craggy old trappers being nice, but the answer had been far from definitive. Her eyes went wide behind her glasses.

To her surprise, he chuckled. "It wasn't. We're just friends." His expression sobered. Propping his elbow on the sofa arm, he pressed his knuckles to his upper lip and mustache. Leah was preparing for another silent spell, when he murmured a muffled, "Until now."

"What do you mean?"

He dropped his hand and took a breath. "Her sending you here. It's beginning to smack of something deliberate."

Leah searched his face for further thoughts. When he didn't answer immediately, she prodded. "I'm listening."

"You said that you never went to Victoria's parties. Did you see her in other social contexts?"

"We went out to dinner often."

"As a foursome—with men?"

"No."

"Did she ever comment on that?"

"She didn't have to. I know that she has male friends, but she loved Arthur very much and has no desire to remarry. She's never at a loss for an escort when the occasion calls for it."

"How about you? *Do* you date?" he asked, repeating the question that had sparked earlier resistance.

Leah answered in a tone that was firm and final. "Not when I can help it."

He was unfazed by her resolve, because he was getting closer to his goal. "Did Victoria have anything to say about that?"

"Oh, yes. She thought I was…working with less than a full deck." Leah grinned at the phrase she had written down moments before, but the grin didn't last. "She was forever trying to fix me up, and I was forever refusing."

Garrick nodded and pressed his lips together, then slid farther down on the sofa, until his thick hair rose against its back. For several more minutes he was lost in thought. Eventually he took a deep breath and raised disheartened eyes to the rafters. "That," he said, "was what I was afraid of."

Not having been privy to his thoughts, Leah didn't follow. "What do you mean?"

"She's done the same to me more than once."

"Done what?"

"Tried to fix me up." He held up a hand. "Granted, it's more difficult up here, but that didn't stop her. She's convinced that anyone who hasn't experienced what she had with Arthur is missing out on life's bounty." His eyes sought Leah's, and he hesitated for a long moment before speaking. "Do you see what I'm getting at?"

With dawning horror, Leah did see. "She did it on purpose."

"Looks that way."

"She didn't tell me about the fire, but she did tell me about you."

"Right."

Closing her eyes, Leah fought a rising anger. "She was so cavalier about my paying rent, wouldn't accept anything beforehand, told me to send her whatever I thought the place was worth."

"Clever."

"When I asked if the cabin was well equipped, her exact words were, 'When last I saw it, it was.'"

"True enough."

"No wonder she was edgy."

"Victoria? Edgy?"

"Unusual, I know, but she was. I chalked it up to a latent maternal instinct." She rolled her eyes. "Boy, was I wrong. It was guilt, pure guilt. She actually had the gall to remind me that I wouldn't have air-conditioning or a phone, the snake." Muttering the last under her breath, Leah turned her back on Garrick and crossed her arms over her breasts.

That was the moment he came to believe that everything she'd told him was the truth. Had she started to shout and pace the floor in anger, he would have wondered. That would have smelled of a script, a soap-opera reaction, lacking subtlety.

But she wasn't shouting or pacing. Her anger was betrayed only by quickened breathing and the rigidity of her stance. From the little he'd seen of her, he'd judged her to be restrained where her emotions were concerned. Her reaction now was consistent with that impression.

Strangely, Garrick's own anger was less acute than he would have expected. If he'd known beforehand what Victoria had planned, he'd have hit the roof. But he hadn't known, and Leah was already here, and there was something about her self-contained distress that tugged at his heart.

Almost before his eyes, that distress turned to mortification. Cheeks a bright red, she cast a harried glance over her shoulder.

"I'm sorry. She had no right to foist me on you."

"It wasn't your fault—"

"But you shouldn't have to be stuck with me."

"It goes two ways. You're stuck with me, too."

"I could have done worse."

"So could I."

Unsure of what to make of his agreeable tone, Leah turned back to the bookshelf. It was then that the full measure of her predicament hit her. She and Garrick had been thrust together for what Victoria had intended to be a romantic spell. But if Victoria had hoped for love at first sight, she was going to be disappointed. Leah didn't believe in love at first sight. She wasn't even sure if she believed in love, since it had brought her pain once before, but that was neither here nor there. She didn't know Garrick Rodenhiser. Talk of love was totally inappropriate.

Attraction at first sight—that, perhaps, was worth considering. She couldn't deny that she found Garrick physically appealing. Not even his sprawling pose could detract from his long-limbed grace. His face, his beard, the sturdiness of his shoulders spoke of ruggedness; she'd have had to be blind not to see it, and dead not to respond.

And that other attraction—the one spawned by the deep, inner feelings that occasionally escaped from his eyes? It baffled her.

"I didn't want this," she murmured to her knotted hands.

From the silence came a quiet, "I know."

"I feel…you must feel…humiliated."

"A little awkward. That's all."

"Here I am in your underwear…"

"You can get dressed if you want."

It was, of course, the wise thing to do. Perhaps, once

she was wearing her own clothes again, she'd feel less vulnerable, less exposed....

Crossing to the dryer, she removed her things and folded them over the crook of her elbow. When she reached for her sweater, though, she found it still damp.

"Here." Garrick stood directly behind her, holding out one of his own sweaters. "Clean and dry."

She accepted it with a quiet thanks and made her escape to the bathroom. He was working at the fireplace when she came out. She suddenly realized that though the fire had gone out during the night, the cabin had stayed warm.

"How do you manage for heat and electricity?" she asked, bracing her hands on the back of the sofa.

He added a final log to the arrangement and reached for a match. "There's a generator out back."

"And food? If you can't get to the store in this weather..."

"I stocked up last week." Sitting back on his heels, he watched the flames take hold. "Anyone who's lived through mud season once knows to be prepared. The freezer is full, and the cabinets. I picked up more fresh stuff a couple of days ago, but I'm afraid the bacon we had for breakfast is the last of it for a while."

He'd have had some left for tomorrow if he hadn't had to share. Leah's feelings of guilt remained unexpressed, though; there was nothing more boring than a person who constantly apologized.

Garrick stood and turned to face her, then wished he hadn't. She was wearing his sweater. It was far too large for her, of course, and she'd rolled the sleeves to a proper length, but the way it fell around her shoulders and breasts was far more suggestive than he'd have dreamed. She looked adorable. And unsure.

He gestured toward the sofa. With a tight smile, she took possession of a corner cushion, drew up her knees and tucked her feet beneath her. That was when he caught sight of the tear in her slacks.

"How's the leg?"

"Okay."

"Did you change the dressing?"

"No."

"Have you looked under it?"

"I'd be able to see if something was oozing through the gauze. Nothing is."

She hadn't looked, he decided. Either she was squeamish, or the gash didn't bother her enough to warrant attention. He wanted to know which it was.

Facing her on the sofa, he eased back the torn knit of her slacks.

"It's fine. Really."

But he was quickly tugging at the adhesive and, less quickly, lifting the gauze. "Doesn't look fine," he muttered. "I'll bet it hurts like hell." With cautious fingertips he probed the angry flesh around the wound. Leah's soft intake of breath confirmed his guess. "It probably should have been stitched, but the nearest hospital's sixty miles away. We wouldn't have made it off the mountain."

"It's not bleeding. It'll be okay."

"You'll have a scar."

"What's one more scar?"

He met her eyes. "You have others?"

Oh, yes, but only one was visible to the naked eye. "I had my appendix out when I was twelve."

He imagined the way her stomach would be, smooth and soft, warm, touchable. When the blood that flowed through his veins grew warmer, he tried to imagine the ugly line marring the flesh, but couldn't. Nor, at that moment, could he tear his eyes from hers.

Pain and loneliness. That was what he saw. She blinked once, as though to will the feelings away, but they remained, swelling against her self-restraint.

He saw, heard, felt. He wanted to ask her, to tell her, to share the pain and ease the burden. He wanted to reach out.

But he didn't.

Instead, he rose quickly and strode off, returning moments later with a tube of ointment and fresh bandages. When he'd dressed the injury to his satisfaction, he replaced the first-aid supplies in the cupboard, took a down vest, then a hooded rain jacket from the closet, stepped into a pair of crusty work boots and went out into the storm.

Leah stared after him, belatedly aware that she was trembling. She didn't understand what had happened just then, any more than she'd understood it when it had happened the night before. His eyes had reflected every one of her emotions. Could he know what she felt?

On a more mundane level, she was puzzled by his abrupt departure, mystified as to where he'd be going in the rain. A short time later she had an answer when a distinct and easily recognizable sound joined that of the steady patter on the roof. She went to the window and peered out. He was across the clearing, chopping wood beneath the shelter of a primitive lean-to.

Smiling at the image of the outdoorsman at work, she

returned to the sofa. While she directed her eyes to the fire, though, she wasn't as successful with her thoughts. She was wondering how the hands of a woodsman, hands that were calloused, fingers that were long and blunt, could be as gentle as they'd been. Richard had never touched her that way, though as her husband, he'd touched her far more intimately.

But there was touching and there was touching, one merely physical, the other emotional, as well. There was something about Garrick…something about Garrick…

Unsettled by her inability to find answers to the myriad questions, she sought diversion in one of the books she'd seen on the shelf. Sheer determination had her surprisingly engrossed in the story when Garrick returned sometime later.

Arms piled high with split logs, he blindly kicked off his boots at the door, deposited the wood in a basket by the hearth, threw back his hood and unbuckled his jacket.

Leah didn't have to ask if the rain had let up. The boots he'd left by the door were covered with mud; his jacket dripped as he shrugged it off.

She returned to her book.

He took up one of his own and sat down.

Briefly she felt the chill he'd brought in. It touched her face, her arm, her leg on the side nearest to him. The fire was warm, though, and the chill soon dissipated.

She read on.

"Do you like it?" he asked after a time.

"It's very well written."

He nodded at that and lowered his eyes to his own book.

Leah had turned several pages before realizing that

he hadn't turned a one. Yet he was concentrating on something....

Craning her neck, she tried to reach the running head at the top of the page. She was beginning to wonder whether she needed a new eyeglass prescription, when he spoke.

"It's Latin."

She smiled. "You're kidding."

"No."

"Are you a Latin scholar?"

"Not yet."

"You're a novice."

"Uh-huh."

Reluctant to disturb him, she returned to her own corner. Studying Latin? That was odd for a trapper, not so odd for a man with a very different past. She would have liked to ask about that past, but she didn't see how she could. He wasn't encouraging conversation. It was bad enough that she was here. The more unobtrusive she was, the better.

Delving into her own book again, she'd read several chapters, when his voice broke the silence.

"Hungry?"

Now that he'd mentioned it... "A little."

"Want some lunch?"

"If I can make it."

"You can't." It was his house, his refrigerator, his food. Given the doubts he'd had about himself since Leah had arrived, he needed to feel in command of something. "Does that mean you won't eat?"

She grimaced. "Got myself into a corner with that one, didn't I?"

"Uh-huh."

"I'll eat."

Trying his best not to smile, Garrick set down his book and went to make lunch. Despite the time he'd spent at the woodshed, he was still annoyed with Victoria. It was difficult, though, to be annoyed with Leah. She was as innocent a pawn in Victoria's game as he was, and, apparently, as uncomfortable with it. But she was a good sport. She conducted herself with dignity. He respected that.

None of the women he'd known in the past would have acceded to as untenable a situation with such grace. Linda Prince would have been livid at the thought of someone isolating her in a secluded cabin. Mona Weston would have been frantic without a direct phone line to her agent. Darcy Hogan would have ransacked his drawers in search of a flattering garment to display her goods. Heather Kane would have screamed at him to stop the rain.

Leah Gates had taken the sweater he offered with gratitude, had found herself a book to read and was keeping to herself.

Which made him all the more curious about her. He wondered what had happened to her marriage and why she didn't date now. He wondered whether she had family, or dreams for the future. He wondered whether the loneliness he saw in her eyes from time to time had to do with the loneliness of this mountainside. Somehow he didn't think so. Somehow he thought the loneliness went deeper. He felt it himself.

Lunch consisted of ham-and-cheese sandwiches on rye. Leah didn't go scurrying for a knife to cut hers in two. She didn't complain about the liberal helping of mayonnaise he'd smeared on out of habit, or about the lettuce and tomato that added bulk and made for a certain sloppiness. She finished every drop of the milk he'd poured without making inane cracks about growing boys and girls or the need for calcium or the marvel of cows. When she'd finished eating, she simply carried both of their plates to the sink, rinsed them and put them in the dishwasher, then returned to the sofa to read.

Midway through a very quiet afternoon, Garrick wasn't concentrating on Latin. He was still thinking of the woman curled in the opposite corner of the sofa. Her legs were tucked beneath her and the book remained open on her lap, but her head had fallen into the crook of the sofa's winged back, and she was sleeping. Silently. Sweetly.

He felt sorry for her. The trip she'd made yesterday—first the drive from New York, then the harrowing hike to his cabin—had exhausted her. He felt a moment's renewed anger toward Victoria for having put her through that ordeal, then realized that Victoria was probably as ignorant of mud season as any other nonnative. Now that he thought of it, she had only been up to the cabin in the best of weather—late spring, summer, early fall.

They'd met for the first time during one of those summer trips, and even then, barely knowing her, he'd asked her why she came at all. She was obviously a city person. She didn't hunt, didn't hike, didn't plant vegetables in a garden behind the cabin. He remembered her response as clearly as if she'd made it yesterday. She had looked him in the eye and told him that the cabin made her feel closer to Arthur. No apology. No bid for sympathy. Just an honest, heartfelt statement of fact that had established the basis of strength and sincerity on which their relationship had bloomed.

Of course, she hadn't been particularly honest in sending Leah to stay in a cabin that didn't exist. He had no doubt, though, that she'd been well-meaning in her desire to get Leah and him together. What puzzled him, irked him, was that she should have known better. He'd fought her in the past. He thought he'd told her enough about himself and his feelings to make himself clear. Why would she think things had changed?

Once upon a time he'd been a city man. He'd lived high and wild. The only things he'd feared in the world had been obscurity and anonymity. Ironically, that very fear had driven him higher and wilder, until he'd destroyed his career and very nearly himself in the process. That was when he'd retreated from the world and sought haven in New Hampshire.

Now he feared everything he'd once prized so dearly. He feared fame because it was fleeting. He feared glory because it was shallow. He feared aggressive crowds because they brought out the worst in human nature, the need for supremacy and domination even on the most mundane of levels.

He'd had it up to his eyeballs with competition. Even after being away from it for four years, he remembered with vile clarity that feeling of itching under the skin, of not being able to sit still and relax for fear someone would overtake him. He couldn't bear the thought of having to be quicker, cruder, more cutthroat than the next. He didn't want to have to worry about how he looked or how he smelled. He didn't want to have to see those younger, more eager actors waiting smugly in the wings for him to falter. And he didn't want the women, clinging like spiders, feeding off him until a sweeter fly came along.

Oh, yes, he knew what he didn't want. He'd made a deliberate intellectual decision when he'd left California. The world of glitz and glamour was behind him, as was the way of life that had had him clawing his way up a swaying ladder. The life he lived here was free of all that. It was simple. It was clean. It was comfortable. It was what he *did* want.

Why, then, did he feel threatened by Leah's presence?

He blinked and realized that she was waking. Rolling slightly, she stretched one leg until the sole of her foot touched his thigh. He felt its warmth and the slight pressure behind it. He saw the way one hand dropped limply to her belly. He watched her turn her head, as though trying to identify the nature of her pillow, then open her eyes with the realization of where she was.

She looked at him. He didn't blink. Slowly, carefully, she drew back her leg and, pushing herself into a seated position, picked up her book and lowered her eyes.

Leah did pose a threat to him, but it wasn't the immediate one of disturbing his peace. She was peaceful herself, quiet, undemanding. No, the threat wasn't a physical one. It was deeply emotional. He looked at her and saw human warmth and companionship—which were the very two things his life lacked. He'd thought he could live without them. Now, for the first time, he wondered.

Leah, too, was pensive. Silently setting her book aside, she went to the window. Rain fell as hard as ever from an endless cloud mass that was heavy and gray. She figured that the rain would last at least through the rest of the day. But even when it stopped—if she'd interpreted Garrick correctly—she wouldn't be immediately on her way. There was the mud to contend with, and if this was mud season, it was possible she'd be here for a while.

Propping her elbows on the window sash, she cupped her chin in her palms and stared out. She could have done worse, she'd told him, and indeed it was so. Garrick Rodenhiser was an easy cabin mate. She was reading, much as she did at home. If she had her dictionaries and thesauruses with her, she could be working much as she did at home. If his pattern of activity on this day was any indication, they could each do their own thing without bothering the other.

The only problem was that he made her think of things she didn't think of when she was at home. He made her think of things she hadn't thought about for years.

Nine years, to be exact. She'd been twenty-four and a graduate student in English when she'd met and married Richard Gates. She'd had dreams then of love and happiness, and she'd been sure that Richard shared them. He was twenty-six when they married and was getting settled in the business world. Or so she'd thought. All too quickly she'd learned that there was nothing "settled" about Richard's view of business. He was on his way to the top, he said, and to get there meant a certain amount of scrambling. It meant temporarily sacrificing a leisurely home life, he said. It meant long days at the office and business trips and parties. Somewhere along the way, love and happiness had been forgotten.

She'd completed her degree but had given up thought of teaching, of course. A working wife hadn't fit into Richard's concept of the corporate life-style. Out of sheer desperation, she'd begun to create crosswords, then had found that she did it well, that she loved it and that there was a ready market for what she composed. Having a career that was part-time and flexible eased some of the frustration she felt.

Perhaps it would have been different if the babies she'd carried had lived. Somehow she doubted it. Richard would have continued on with the work he adored, the business trips and the parties. And why not? He was good at it. There was a charismatic quality to him that drew people right and left. Even aside from the issue of children, she and Richard were in different leagues.

Now, though, she was thinking of love and happiness. She was thinking of the life she'd lived in New York since the divorce. It had seemed fine and comfortable and rewarding…until now.

Garrick affected her. He made her think that there had been something wrong with that single life in New York because it was…single. Seeing him, sitting with him, being touched by those hazel and silver eyes, she sensed what she'd missed. He made her feel lonely. He made her ache for something more than what she'd had.

Was it because she was in a strange place? Was it because her life had been turned upside down? Was it because she didn't know where she was going from here?

He made her think of the future. Yes, she'd probably go back to New York, search for and find another apartment. She'd work; she'd visit friends; she'd go to restaurants and museums and parks. She'd do what she'd always found so comfortable. Why, then, did there seem a certain emptiness to it?

With a sigh of confusion, she returned to the sofa and her book, though she read precious little in the hours that passed. From time to time she felt Garrick's eyes on her. From time to time she looked at him. His presence was both comfort and torment.

He made her feel less alone because he was there, because he'd help her, she knew, if something happened. He made her feel more alone because he was there, because the power of his quiet presence reminded her of everything she'd once wanted and needed.

Garrick went out again late in the afternoon. This time Leah had no clue to his purpose. She wandered around the cabin while he was gone, feeling a restlessness that she couldn't explain any more than she could those other feelings she'd glimpsed.

When he returned, he started making dinner. Once again he refused her offer of help. They ate in silence, occasionally glancing at each other, always looking away when their eyes met. After they'd finished, they returned to the fire. This time, despite the fact that she was without resource books, Leah worked with pad and pencil, sketching out simple puzzles. Garrick whittled.

She wondered where he'd learned to whittle, how he did it, what he was making—but she didn't ask.

He wondered where she started a puzzle, how she got

the words to mesh, what she did at an impasse—but he didn't ask.

By ten o'clock she was feeling tired and frustrated and distinctly out of sorts. Crumpling up a piece of paper, on which she'd created nothing worth saving, she tossed it into the dying fire, then took a shower, put on the long underwear that seemed as good a pair of pajamas as any and climbed onto the same side of the bed where she'd slept the night before.

By ten-thirty, Garrick was feeling tired and frustrated and distinctly out of sorts. Flipping his piece of wood, out of which he'd whittled nothing worth saving, into the nearly dead fire, he turned off the lights, stripped down to his underwear and climbed onto his own side of the bed.

He lay on his back, wide-awake. He thought of L.A. and the day, several months before he'd left, that he'd finally tracked down his agent. Timothy Wilder had been avoiding him. Phone calls had gone unanswered; each time Garrick had shown up at his office, Wilder had been "out." But Garrick had finally located him on the set of a TV movie, where another of Wilder's clients was at work. It hadn't done Garrick any good. Wilder had barely acknowledged him. The director and crew, many of whom he'd worked with in the past, couldn't have been bothered asking how he was. Wilder's client, the star of the show, hadn't given him so much as a glance. And the woman who, six months before, had sworn she adored Garrick, turned her back and walked away. He'd never felt so alone in his life.

Leah, too, lay on her back, wide-awake. She thought of one of the last parties she'd gone to as Richard's wife.

It had been a gala charity function, and she'd taken great care to look smashing. Richard hadn't noticed. Nor had any of the others present. For a time, Richard had towed her from group to group, but then he'd left her to exchange inanities with an eighty-year-old matron. She'd never felt so alone in her life.

Garrick shifted his legs, his gaze on the darkened rafters overhead. He thought of the days following his accident, the three long weeks he'd lain in the hospital. No one had visited. No one had sent cards or flowers. No one had called to cheer him up. Though he fully blamed himself for his downfall and knew that he didn't deserve anyone's sympathy, what he would have liked, could have used, was a little solace. A little understanding. A little encouragement. The fact that it never materialized was the final sorrow.

Leah, too, shifted slightly. She thought of the hours she'd lain in the hospital following the loss of her second child. Richard had made the obligatory visits, but she'd come to dread them, for he clearly saw her as a failure. She'd felt like one, too, and though the doctors assured her that there was nothing more she could have possibly done, she'd been distraught. Had her parents been alive, they'd have been by her side. Had she had her own friends, ones who'd cared for her more than they'd cared for appearances, she mightn't have felt so utterly empty. But her parents were dead, and her "friends" were Richard's. Sorrow had been her sole companion.

Garrick took a deep, faintly shuddering breath. He felt Leah beside him, heard the slight irregularity of her own breathing. Slowly, cautiously, he turned his head on the pillow.

The cabin was dark. He couldn't see her. But he heard a soft swish when her head turned toward his.

They lay that way for long moments. Tension strummed between them, a wire of need, vibrating, pulling. Each held back, held back, fought the magnetism drawing them together until, at last, it became too great.

It wasn't a question of one moving first. In a simultaneous turning, their bodies came together as their minds had already done. Their arms wound around each other. Their legs tangled.

And they clung to each other. Silently. Soulfully.

4

Leah closed her eyes and greedily immersed herself in Garrick's strength. He was warm and alive, and the way he held her confirmed his own need for the closeness she so badly craved. His face was buried in her hair. His arms trembled as they crushed her to him, but not for a minute did she mind the pressure. Instead her own arms tightened around his neck, and she sighed softly in relief.

And pleasure. His body was a marvel. It was long and firm, accommodating itself to fit her perfectly. Richard had never accommodated himself to fit her either physically or emotionally. The fact that Garrick, who owed her nothing, should do so with such sweetness was a wonder she couldn't begin to analyze.

Not that she tried very hard. She was too busy absorbing the comfort he offered to think of much of anything except prolonging it. One of her legs slid deeper between his. Her fingers wound into his hair and held.

Garrick, too, was inundated with gratifying sensations. He felt Leah from head to toe and drank in her softness as though he'd lived through a drought. In a sense he had. From birth. His parents had been wonderful people, but they'd both been professionals, engrossed in their careers, and they'd had neither time nor warmth to give to their son. Had he been born with the need for physical closeness? Had he been born a toucher? If so, it explained why he'd turned to women from the time he'd had something to offer. Only that hadn't fully satisfied him, either, because even at fourteen he'd been ambitious. He'd been always angling for something bigger and better, never taking stock of what he had, never quite appreciating it.

Until now. Holding Leah Gates in his arms, he felt a measure of fullness that he'd never experienced before. He moved his hands along her spine. He rubbed his thigh against her hip. He inhaled, heightening the pressure of his chest against her breasts.

She needed him. The soft, purring sounds she made from time to time told him so. She needed him, but not because he would be a notch in her belt, or because he could further her career, or because he had money. She didn't know who he was and where he'd been, yet she still needed him. For *him*.

The moan that rumbled from his chest was one of sheer gratitude.

For a long, long time, they lay wrapped in each other's arms. Their closeness was a healing balm, blotting out memories of past pain and sorrow. Nothing existed but the present, and it was so soothing that neither would have thought to disturb it.

Ironically, what disturbed it was the very solace it brought. For with the edge taken off emptiness came a new awareness. It struck Leah gradually—a pleasantly male and musky scent filtering into her nostrils, the thick silk of hair sifting through her fingers, the swell of muscles flexing beneath her arm. On his part, Garrick grew conscious of a clean, womanly fragrance, the gentleness of the curves that his palms rounded, the heat that beckoned daringly close to his loins.

He hadn't been thinking of sex when he'd taken Leah in his arms. He'd simply wanted to hold her and be held back. He'd wanted, for however fleeting the moments, to binge on the nearness of another human being. But his body was insistent. His heart had begun to beat louder, his blood to course faster, his muscles to grow tighter. He'd never been hit by anything as unexpectedly—or as desperately.

He might have restrained himself if Leah hadn't begun, in wordless ways, to tell him how she wanted him, too. Her hands had slipped down his back and were furrowing beneath his thermal top, gliding upward along his flesh. Her breathing was more shallow. Her breasts swelled against him. He might have called all that simply an extension of the act of holding had it not been for the faint but definitely perceptible arching of her hips.

Or was the arching his? His lower body, with a will of its own, was pressing into her heat, then undulating slowly, then needing even more. He, too, was exploring beneath thermal, only his hands had forayed below Leah's waist and were clenching the firm flare of her bottom, holding her closer, increasing the friction, adding to a hunger that was already explosive.

He had to have her. He had to bury himself in her depths, because he needed that closeness, too, and he was frightened that he'd lose it if he waited.

With hands that shook, he pushed her bottoms to her knees. She squirmed free of them while he lowered his own. Her thigh was already lifting over his when he began his penetration, and by the time he was fully sheathed, she was digging her fingers into his back and sighing softly against his neck.

It was fast and mutual. He stroked deeply and with growing speed. She matched each stroke in pace and ardor. He gasped and quivered. She gulped and shivered. Then they surged against each other a final time, and their bodies erupted into simultaneous spasms. Totally earth-shattering. Endlessly fulfilling. Warm and wet and wonderful.

Garrick's heart thundered long after. His breath came in ragged pants that would have embarrassed him had not Leah been equally as winded. He thought about withdrawing, then thought again, reluctant to leave her when he felt so incredibly contained and content. So he stayed where he was until he began to fear that he was hurting her. But when he made to move away, she clutched him tighter.

"Don't go!" she whispered.

They were the sweetest after-love words he'd ever heard. Not only did they tell him that she savored the continuing contact, they also said something about her feelings toward what they'd just shared.

They reassured him, too. He hadn't performed in a particularly skillful way. He hadn't coaxed her, caressed her, teased her into a state of arousal. He hadn't spoken. He hadn't even kissed her. But she'd been ready.

Because she'd needed him. Because she hadn't had a man in a long time. Because it had been more than sex. And because she, too, had felt its uniqueness.

He didn't say anything when he felt the tremors in her body and realized that she was crying. He spoke with his hands, curving one around her neck to keep her pressed close, using the other to gently stroke her hair. He knew why she was crying, and he felt it, too. But he felt more—a protectiveness that kept his movements steady and soothing until, at length, she cried herself to sleep. Only then did he close his eyes as well.

Consciousness came slowly to Leah the next morning. She was first aware of being delightfully warm. Drawing her knees closer, she snuggled beneath the thick quilt. With a lazy yawn, she discovered that she felt rested. And satisfied. Her limbs were relaxed, almost languid, but there was a fullness inside that hadn't been there before.

Then she realized that she was wearing nothing from the waist down, and her eyes opened.

Garrick was sitting on the side of the bed. On her side. He was fully dressed. And he was watching her.

Not quite sure what to say, she simply looked at him.

Gently and with a slight hesitance, he smoothed a strand of dark hair from her cheek and tucked it behind her ear. "Are you okay?"

She nodded.

His voice dropped to a whisper. "I didn't hurt you?"

She shook her head.

"Any regrets?"

She spoke as softly as he had. "No."

"I'm glad." His hand fell back to the quilt. "Hungry?"

"Famished."

"Could you eat some pancakes?"

"Very easily."

A tiny smile broke out on his face. She would have reached for her glasses to better see and enjoy it, but she didn't want to move an inch.

"How 'bout I make a double batch while you get dressed?"

"Sounds fair."

He squeezed her shoulder lightly through the quilt before leaving to fulfill his half of the bargain. Only when she heard busy sounds coming from the kitchen did she pay heed to her half. Rooting around between the sheets, she found and managed to struggle into her thermal bottoms. Once in the bathroom, she showered and dressed, then returned to the main room, where Garrick was adding the last of the pancakes to high stacks on each of two plates.

"Real syrup," she observed after she'd sat down. "This is a luxury."

He watched her dribble it sparingly atop the pancakes, then ordered quietly, "More."

"But it's too good to waste."

"There's no waste if you enjoy it. Besides, this is last year's batch. The new stuff will be along in another month."

Leah turned the plastic container in her hand. It had no label. "Is this local?"

"Very."

"You made it yourself?"

He shook his head. "I don't have the equipment."

"I thought all you had to do was to stick a little spigot in a tree."

"That's true, in a sense. But if you stick one little spigot in one tree, then take the sap you get and boil it down into syrup, you get just about enough to sprinkle on a single pancake."

"Oh."

"Exactly. What you have to do is tap many trees, preferably have long hoses carrying the sap directly to a sugar house, then boil it all in huge vats. There are many people in the area who do it that way. I get my syrup from a family that lives on the other side of town."

"Do they make syrup for a living?"

"They earn some money from it, but not enough to support them. The season's pretty limited."

She nodded in understanding, but her appreciation wasn't as much for the information as for the fact that he'd offered it willingly. Up until now they'd exchanged few words. She realized that, living alone, he wasn't used to talking. Still, while she'd been showering she'd wondered whether there would be awkward silences between them, given what had happened last night. She'd meant what she'd said; she had no regrets. But she hadn't asked him if he did.

From his relaxed manner, she guessed that he didn't, and it pleased her. Turning her attention to her pancakes, she cut off a healthy forkful. Her fork wavered just above the plate, though, and she stared at it.

"Garrick?"

His mouth was full. "Mmm?"

"I just wanted to say…I wanted to tell you…what happened last night…well, I haven't ever done anything like that before."

He swallowed what was in his mouth. "I know."

Her eyes met his. "You do?"

"You were tight. You haven't made love in a long time. Not since your divorce?"

Cheeks pink, she shook her head in affirmation. "I wanted to make sure you knew. I didn't want you to get the wrong impression. I mean, I don't regret for a minute what we did, but I'm not the kind of woman who just jumps into bed with a man."

"I know—"

"But I wasn't sex starved—"

"I know—"

"And it wasn't just because you were there—"

"I know—"

"Because I don't believe in casual affairs—"

"I know—"

Setting down her fork, she curved her fingers against her bangs. "This is coming out wrong. Now it sounds as though I'm rigidly principled and expect something from you, but that isn't it at all."

"I know. Leah? If you don't eat, the pancakes will get cold."

"I'm not a prude *or* a sex fiend. It's just that last night I needed you—"

"Leah…" He focused pointedly on her plate.

She gave up trying to explain and set to eating. All she could do was hope that he'd understood what she'd been trying to say. She cared what he thought of her, and though part of her was sure he'd known what she'd been feeling last night another part was less confident.

Confidence was something she lacked where relationships with men were concerned. She'd thought she'd known what Richard had wanted, and she'd been wrong. But that was only one of the reasons she'd avoided men since her divorce.

She avoided them because she was independent for the first time in her life and was enjoying it. She avoided them because she always had and always would detest the dating ritual. She avoided them because none of the men she met sparked the slightest romantic interest. And she avoided them because she had a fair idea of what a man had in mind when he asked out a thirty-three-year-old divorcée.

Yes, she cared about what Garrick thought of her, but before that—and more so now than ever—she cared what she thought about herself. She wasn't a tramp. She wasn't out for gratuitous sex. She liked to think of herself as a woman of pride, a selective woman. She liked to think that when she did something, she did it with good reason.

That had been the case in bed last night. From the first she'd felt an affinity for Garrick. Above and beyond what Victoria had said, her instincts had told her much about the kind of man he was. He wasn't a playboy. Just as he'd known she hadn't made love in a while, she knew the same about him. There was nothing in his cabin—no leftover lingerie, no perfume or errant earrings stuck in a corner of the medicine chest—to suggest that he'd had a woman here. The urgency with which he'd entered her and so quickly climaxed was telling.

Indefinite periods of celibacy notwithstanding, he was all man, ruggedness incarnate. From the way his sandy-gray hair fell randomly over his brow, to the way his beard grew, to his pantherlike gait, to his capacity for chopping and carting wood, he was the kind of macho hero too often limited to the silver screen.

Macho ended, though, with his looks and carriage. He was a three-dimensional man, capable of gentleness and consideration. Those qualities were the ones that had gotten to her first. They were, ironically, the ones that had evoked such a tremendous surge of emotion within her—emotion that had, in the final analysis, been the reason she'd made love with him.

It hadn't been simply because he was there. If he'd been cruel or unfeeling, repulsive either physically or emotionally, she'd never have climbed into his bed, much less made love with him, regardless of the depth of her need. No, she'd sought comfort from him because he was Garrick. He was a man she could probably love, given the inclination and time.

Of course, she had neither, and thought of the time brought her back to the present. Swishing the last piece of pancake around in the remaining drops of syrup, she brought it to her mouth and ate it, then put down her fork and looked toward the window.

"It's still raining, isn't it?" She'd gotten so used to the sound on the roof that she practically didn't hear it.

Garrick, who'd finished well before her, had his chair braced back on its rear legs. He was nursing the last of his coffee. "Uh-huh."

"No sign of a letup?"

"Nope."

It occurred to her that she wasn't as disappointed about that as she might have been, and she felt guilty. Despite all that had happened, she was still imposing on Garrick. "No hope of getting to my car?" she forced herself to ask.

He shrugged. The front legs of his chair met the floor with a soft thud, and he stood, gathering the dishes together. "I was thinking of making a try later. You'd probably like some other clothes."

He hadn't said anything about freeing the car or getting rid of her. She smiled and, looking down, plucked at the voluminous folds of his sweater. "I don't know. I'm beginning to get used to this. It's comfortable."

Garrick wasn't sure he'd ever get used to how great she looked. When he'd first seen her in it, he'd thought she looked adorable. Now, having had the intense pleasure of being inside her, he thought she looked sexy. That went for the way she looked in his thermal long johns, too. He hadn't thought so at first, but he'd changed his mind, and his body wasn't about to let him change it back.

Taking refuge at the sink, he began to clean up with more energy than was strictly necessary. It helped. By the time he was done, he had his libido in check. He didn't want to frighten Leah or act as though she should pay for her keep by satisfying his every urge. And it wasn't as if his every urge *was* for sex, though after last night, he had a greater inclination toward it than he'd had in years.

Last night…last night had been very, very special. It was sex, but it wasn't. It was so much an emotional act, rather than a physical one, that he didn't have the words to describe it. Yes, if there were to be a repeat, the emotional element would be present, but he knew that there'd be more. He knew that this time he'd want to touch her and kiss her. This time he'd want to explore her body and get to know it as completely as, in some ways, he felt he knew her soul. Her mind, ah, that was another matter. He wanted to get to know it, too, but…probably that wasn't wise. When the ground dried up, she'd be leaving. He didn't want to miss her.

Which was why he reverted into the silence with which he'd grown increasingly comfortable over four years' time. He didn't ask her any of the million questions he had. He told himself he didn't want to know the details of what made Leah Gates tick. If he didn't know it would be easier to pretend that she was shallow and boring. Easier to tell himself, when she was gone, that he was better off without her.

Leah spent the morning much as she had her waking hours the day before. She finished one book and started another. She made frequent notes on a pad of paper when she encountered a word or concept in her reading that would translate into a crossword. She doodled out nonsense puzzles, but the puzzle that commanded her real interest was Garrick.

He was an enigma. She knew that they had at least one need in common, and she knew, in general, the type of man he was. The specifics of his day-to-day life, though, were a mystery, as was his past.

Mentally she'd outlined a crossword puzzle. Garrick's name was blocked in, as were certain other facts pertaining to their relationship, but she needed more information if she hoped to find the words to complete the grid.

It was late morning. They were each sitting in what she'd come to think of as their own little corner of the sofa. Garrick had gone outside for a while, though not to the car, he'd told her when she'd asked. He hadn't elaborated further, and she'd been loath to press. It was his home. He was free to come and go as he pleased. She couldn't help but be curious, though, particularly when he returned after no more than thirty minutes.

After letting him dry off and settle in with his book for a while, she ventured to satisfy her curiosity.

"I hope I'm not keeping you from doing things."

"You're not."

"What would you be doing if I weren't here?"

"On a day like this, not much of anything."

Which was precisely what he was doing now, he mused a tad wryly. He'd gone to the back shed, thinking that working with toothpicks and glue, making progress on the model home he'd been commissioned to make, would be therapeutic. But if the therapy had been intended to take his mind off Leah, it had failed. Even the book that lay open on his lap—a novel he'd purchased the week before—failed to capture him.

Leah broke into his thoughts. "And if it weren't raining?"

"I'd be outside."

"Trapping?"

He shrugged.

"Victoria said you were a trapper."

"I am, but the best part of the trapping season's over for the year."

She let that statement sink in, but it raised more questions than it answered. So a while later, she tried again.

"What do you trap?"

He was crouching before the fire, adding another log to the flames. "Fisher, fox, raccoon."

"You sell the furs?"

He hesitated, wondering if Leah was the crusader type who'd lecture him about the evils of killing animals to provide luxury items for rich people. He decided that there was only one way to find out.

"That's right."

"I've never owned a fur coat."

"Why not?" He turned on his haunches, waiting for the lecture.

"They're too expensive, for one thing. Richard—my ex-husband—thought I should have one, but I kept putting him off. If you walk into a restaurant with a fur, either you're afraid to check it in case it gets stolen, or the management refuses to *let* you check it. In either case, you have to spend the evening worrying about whether your *fruits de mer au chardonnay* will spatter. Besides, I've always thought fur coats to be too showy. And they're heavy. I don't want that kind of weight on my shoulders."

It wasn't quite the answer Garrick had feared, but it was a fearful one nonetheless, for it had given him a glimpse of her life—at least, the one she'd had when she'd been married. Her husband had apparently been well-to-do. They'd gone to fine French restaurants and had kept company with women who *did* worry about spattering sauce on their furs. If he could tell himself that Leah was as turned off by that kind of life-style as he was, he'd feel better. He'd also feel worse, because he'd like her even more.

"I see your point" was all he said, returning to the sofa and lowering his eyes to his book in hopes of ending the conversation. Leah took the hint and said nothing more, but *that* bothered him. If she'd pushed, he might have had something to hold against her. He hated pushy women, and Lord, had he known his share.

Lunchtime came. Halfway through her bologna sandwich, Leah set it down gently. "Did I offend you?"

"Excuse me?"

"When I said that I didn't like fur coats?"

He'd been deep in his own musings, which had gone far beyond fur coats. It took him a minute to return. "You didn't offend me. I don't like them, either."

"No?"

He shook his head.

"Doesn't that take some of the pleasure out of your work?"

"How so?"

"Having someone turn the product of your hard work into something you don't like? I know I'd be devastated if someone used my page of the paper to wrap fish."

"Does anyone?"

"I've never witnessed it personally, but I'm sure it's been done more than once."

"If you see it, what would you do?"

She considered for a minute, then gave a half shrug. "Rationalize, I suppose."

"How?"

"I'd tell myself that I enjoyed creating the puzzle and that I was paid for it, but that…that's the end of my involvement. If it gives someone pleasure to wrap fish in my puzzle—" she hesitated, hating to say the next but knowing she had to "—so be it."

He grinned.

She winced, then murmured sheepishly, "If it gives someone pleasure to wear a fur coat, so be it…." She tucked her hair behind her ear. "Do you enjoy trapping?"

"Yes."

"Why?"

"It takes skill."

"You like the challenge."

"Yes."

"Where did you learn how to do it?"

"A trapper taught me." He stood and reached across the table for her plate. "All done?"

She nodded. "A local trapper?"

"He's dead now." Stacking the plates together, balancing glasses and flatware on top, he carried the lot to the sink. "I thought I'd make a stab at reaching your car. If you tell me what you want, I'll bring back as much as I can."

She rose quickly. "I'll come with you."

"No."

"Two pairs of hands are better than one."

He turned to face her. "Not in this case. If I have to hold you with one arm, I'll have only one left for your things."

"You won't have to hold me."

"Come on, Leah. You've been through that muck once. You know how treacherous it is."

She approached the sink, intent on making her point. "But that was at night. I couldn't see. I didn't know where I was going. My shoes weren't the greatest—"

"What shoes would you wear now?"

"Yours. You must have an old pair of boots lying around."

"Sure. Size twelve."

She was standing directly before him, her face bright with hope. "I could pad them with wool socks."

"You could also pack your feet in cement and try to move, because that's pretty much what it would be like."

"I could do it, Garrick."

"Not fast enough. In case you've forgotten, it's raining out there. The idea is to make the round trip as quickly as possible."

"How long can it take to dash a mile?"

"A mile?" He laughed. "Is that how far you thought you'd gone?"

"It took me forever," she reasoned defensively, then quickly added, "but that was because it was dark and I kept falling."

"Well, it's light now, but you'll fall anyway, because it's slippery as hell out there. I'm used to it." He brushed a forefinger along his mustache. "By the way, Victoria's cabin is just about a third of a mile from here."

"A *third*—" she began in amazement, then turned embarrassment into optimism. "But that's *nothing*. I'll be able to do it."

Garrick looked down at her. Her head was tipped back, her brows arched high in hope. He found himself caught, enchanted by the gentle color on her cheeks, taunted by her moist, slightly parted lips. He wanted to kiss her just then, wanted it so suddenly and so badly that he knew he couldn't do it. He'd bruise her. He'd be settling an argument in the sexist way he'd used in the past but detested now. Worse, he'd be showing a decided lack of control.

Control was what his new life was about. Self-control. No drinking, no smoking, no carousing. No impulsive kisses.

Instead of lowering his mouth to hers, he raised his hands to her shoulders and held them lightly. "I'd rather you stay here, Leah. For your own safety and comfort, if nothing else."

Had he said it any other way or offered any other reason, Leah probably would have continued to argue. But his voice had been like smooth sand in the sun, fine grains of warmth entering her, quieting her, and his expression of concern was new and welcome.

Sucking on her upper lip, she stepped back, then forward again, this time around his large frame. She gave him a gentle nudge at the back of his waist. "Go. I'll clean up."

"You'll have to tell me what you want."

"Let me think for a minute."

While she thought, he built up the fire and pulled on his rain gear. He was just finishing buckling his boots, when she handed him a list of what she'd like and where in her car he could find it. Tucking that list into the pocket of his oilskin slicker, he tugged up the hood, tipped its rim in the facsimile of a salute, then left.

A short time later, sitting in the driver's seat of the Golf, Garrick drew Victoria's letter from Leah's purse. He held it, turned it, stared at the back flap. He should slit it open, but he didn't want to. He knew that he'd find an enthusiastic recommendation of Leah, and he certainly didn't need that. Leah was doing just fine on her own behalf.

Damn, Victoria!

Stuffing the letter back into the purse, he quickly collected the things Leah had requested. It was an easy task, actually. She was very organized. Her note was even funny.

Battered Vuitton duffel (a gift, not my style) on top of no-name suitcases behind passenger's seat. Mickey Mouse bookbag, one across and two down from duffel. Large grocery sack behind driver's seat. (If sack reeks, scatter contents for animals and take black canvas tote bag, riding shotgun, instead.)

The sack didn't reek, and he was able to manage the tote, too. He felt a little foolish with a purse slung over his shoulder, but it was well hidden by the rest of the load, and besides, who would see him?

No one did see him, but as he slogged through the rain heading back toward the cabin, he grew more and more annoyed. He was peeved at Leah for being so sweet and alone and comfortable. He was put out with Victoria for having sent her to him in the first place. He was riled by the bundles he carried, for they swung against his sides and made the task of keeping his balance on the slick mud that much harder. He was irritated with the rain, which trickled up his cuffs and which, if it hadn't come at all, would have spared him the larger mess he was in.

Mostly he was angry at life for throwing him a curve when he least expected or needed it. Things had been going so well for him. He had his head straight, his priorities set. Then Leah came along, and suddenly he saw voids where he hadn't seen them before.

He wanted her with a vengeance, and that infuriated him. She was a threat to the way of life he'd worked so hard to establish, because he sensed that nothing would be the same when she left. And she would leave. She was city. She was restaurants and theater and Louis Vuitton luggage—even if it *had* been a gift. She wasn't about to fit into his life-style for long. Oh, sure, she found it a novelty now. The leisurely pace and the quiet were a break from her regular routine. But she'd be bored before long. So she'd leave. And he'd be alone again. Only this time he'd mind it.

By the time he reached the cabin he was in a dark mood. After silently depositing his load, he went out again and hiked farther up the mountain, moving quickly, ignoring the rain and cold. He felt a little more in control of himself when he finally turned and began the descent, but even then he bought extra time by going to the shed to work.

It was late when he entered the cabin. Leah had turned on the lights, and the fire was burning brightly. But it wasn't the smell of wood smoke that met him. Shrugging from his wet outerwear, he sniffed the air, then glowered toward the kitchen.

Leah was at the stove. She'd looked up when he'd stomped in, but her attention had quickly returned to whatever it was she was stirring. He didn't recognize the pan as one of his own, though he hadn't been that long from civilization not to recognize it as a wok.

"Chinese?" he warbled. "You're cooking Chinese?"

She sent him a nervous glance. "I'm trying. I just finished taking a course in it, but I haven't really done it on my own. It was one of the things I was going to play with at Victoria's cabin." What was apparently an in-struction book lay open on the counter beside her, but Garrick wasn't up for marveling at Leah's industrious-ness.

"You mean—I was hauling Chinese groceries in that sack?"

"Among other things." Many of which she'd quickly put in the freezer, others of which were refrigerated, a few of which she'd questioned and thrown out.

"And a *wok?* I thought I was bringing you *essentials.*"

She shot him a second, even more nervous glance. He was angry. She had no idea why. "You asked me to tell you what I wanted. These were some of the things."

He looked around for the other bags he'd carried, but they'd apparently been unloaded and stored—some-where. Planting his hands on his hips, he glared at her. "What else did I cart through the rain?"

His tone was so reminiscent of the imperious one Richard had often used that Leah had to struggle not to cringe. She kept her voice steady, but it was small. "The wok. It was with my books in the Mickey Mouse bag. And some clothes." She spared a fast glance at the faded jeans she'd put on. "I threw out the torn slacks. They were hopeless." She was also wearing a pair of well-worn moc-casins that had been in the duffel, but she hadn't changed out of Garrick's sweater. Now she wished she had.

"What was in the black tote? It was heavy as hell."

At that moment, Leah would have given anything to be able to lie. She'd never been good at it; her eyes gave her away. Not that lying would have done any good in this case, since he would learn the truth soon enough.

"A cassette player and tapes," she mumbled.

"A *what?*"

She looked him in the eye and said more clearly, "A cassette player and tapes."

"Oh-ho, no, you don't! You're not going to disturb my peace and quiet with raucous music!"

"It's not raucous."

"Then loud. I didn't come up here to put up with *that.*"

Leah knew she should indulge him. After all, it was his cabin and he was doing her a favor by taking her in. But there'd been so much more between them that having him shout at her only raised her hackles. She'd heard enough shouting from Richard. When they divorced, she'd vowed never to be the butt of unreasonable mood swings again.

She'd thought Garrick was different.

"I'll play it softly, or not at all while you're here," she stated firmly, "but if you're gone for hours like you were today, I'll enjoy it any way I want."

"It bothered you that I left you alone, did it?" he demanded.

"It did not! You can go where you want, when you want and for however long you want. But if you're not here, I'll listen to my music. And anyway, in a few days I'll be gone." She took a shaky breath. "I may be invading your privacy, but, don't forget, if it hadn't been for you Victoria would have never sent me up here!"

That took Garrick aback. He hadn't thought of it quite that way, but Leah had a point. For that matter, Leah often had a point and it was usually reasonable. Which made him feel all the more unreasonable.

Wheeling away, he strode off to hang his wet jacket on a hook, then marched back to the dresser by the bed, yanked his turtleneck jersey and heavy wool sweater over his head in one piece, tossed them heedlessly aside and began tugging out drawers in search of a replacement.

Leah's throat went positively dry as she stared after him. All anger was forgotten in the face of his nakedness. Granted, it was only his back, but his cords hung low on his hips, presenting her with a view of skin that was breathtaking. There was nothing burly about his shoulders. They were broad, but every inch was hard flesh over corded sinew. The same was true of his arms and, for that matter, the rest of his torso. There wasn't a spare ounce of fat in sight. His spine bisected symmetrical pockets of muscle that stretched and flexed as he bent over and tore through the drawer. His waist was lean, the skin there smooth. He wasn't tanned, though she guessed that once the spring sun came he would be. He struck her as a man who'd be outside in good weather, shirtless.

Her insides burned, but jerking her eyes back to the contents of the wok, she realized with relief that that was all that had. She set the cover on the shallow pan with a hand that trembled, turned off the propane gas, then lifted the cover from a second pan, one of Garrick's, and checked the rice.

Everything was ready. The food was cooked. The table was set. And Garrick was slouched on the sofa, wearing a battered sweatshirt, taking his sour mood out on the fire.

She debated leaving him alone. She could dish out

the food and sit down. Surely he'd see that dinner was on the table and join her. Or would he?

Her approach was quiet and hesitant. "Garrick?"

His mouth rested against a fist. "Mmm?"

"I'm all set. If you're hungry." She pressed her damp palms to her jeans.

"Ydnnvtmakdnnn."

"Excuse me?"

He raised his fist, but his words remained low and begrudging. "You didn't have to make dinner."

"I know."

"What is it, anyway?"

"Braised chicken with black beans."

He didn't take his eyes from the fire. "I haven't had Chinese food in four years. I've always hated it."

Feeling inexplicably hurt, Leah turned away. She wasn't all that hungry herself, all of a sudden, but she had no intention of letting her efforts go to waste. So she prepared a plate for herself, sat down and began to eat.

Out of the corner of her eye she saw Garrick rise from the sofa. He went to the stove, clattered covers and sniffed loudly. She was struggling to swallow a small cube of chicken, when she heard the distinct sounds of food being dished out. The chicken slid down more easily.

Moments later, he took his place across from her. She didn't look up but continued to eat, though she couldn't have described what she was tasting.

"Not bad," Garrick conceded. His normally raspy voice was gruffer than normal. He took another bite, chewed and swallowed. "What's in it?"

"Ginger root, bamboo shoots, scallions, oyster sauce, sherry…"

"Not the kind of stuff that comes in cardboard take-out containers."

"No." She took a minute to concentrate on what she was eating and, to her relief, agreed with his assessment. It was good. She had nothing to be ashamed of, and that mattered to her, where Garrick was concerned. It was the first time she'd cooked for him. As a matter of pride, she'd wanted the results to be highly palatable.

They ate in silence. More than once, Leah had to bite her tongue to keep from voicing the questions on her mind. She wanted to know why he'd been so angry, what she'd done to cause it. She wanted to know what he had against music. She wanted to know when he'd eaten Chinese food from takeout containers and why he'd developed such an aversion to it. And she wanted to know where he'd been and what he'd been doing four years ago.

He didn't offer any further conversation, though, and she didn't dare start any for fear of setting him off. She liked the Garrick who was quiet and gentle, not the one who brooded darkly, or worse, growled at her.

She had no way of knowing that, at that moment, Garrick was disliking himself. He was disgusted with the way he'd behaved earlier, though his present behavior was only a marginal improvement. But he couldn't seem to help himself. The more he saw of Leah, the more he liked her, and paradoxically, the more he resented her.

Chinese food. The mere words conjured up images of late nights on the set, where dinner was wolfed out of cartons scattered along an endless table at the rear of the studio. He'd barely known what he was eating. His stomach had inevitably been upset long before, and the best he'd been able to do was to wash whatever it was down with swigs of Scotch.

Chinese food. Another image came to mind, this one of a midnight date with a willowy blonde who'd been good enough to pick up the food on her way over to his place. He wouldn't have bothered to pick *her* up. He'd known what she'd wanted and he'd delivered—crudely and with little feeling. The next morning, more than a little hung over, he'd retched at the smell of the food that remained in the cartons.

Chinese food. One last image. He'd been alone. No work, no friends. He'd been high on something or other, and he'd gone to the takeout counter and ordered enough for twelve, supposedly to look as though he were having a party. As though he were still important, still a star. He'd gone home, sat in his garish living room, stared at the leather sofas and the huge bags of food and had bawled like a baby.

"Garrick?"

Leah's voice brought him back. His head shot up just as she passed an envelope across the table. Victoria's letter. He glared at it for a minute before snatching it from her fingers. The legs of his chair scraped against the floor. He crossed the room quickly, slapped the unopened letter onto the top of the dresser, then dropped back into the sofa and resumed his brooding.

Quietly Leah began to clear the table. Her movements were slow, her shoulders slumped in defeat. It wasn't the meal that caused her discouragement; she knew it had been good and that for a time Garrick had enjoyed what he'd eaten. She couldn't even take offense at his brusque departure, because she knew he was hurting. She'd seen his eyes grow distant, seen the pain they'd held. Oh, yes, she knew he was hurting, but she didn't know what to do about it, and that was the cause of her distress. She wanted to reach out, but she was afraid. She felt totally impotent.

When there was nothing left to do in the kitchen, she picked up a book—one of her own—and as unobtrusively as possible slid into her corner of the sofa. She couldn't read, though. She was too aware of Garrick.

An hour passed. He looked at her. "You said there were clothes in the bag I brought."

She glanced down at her jeans, then her moccasins.

"Besides those," he muttered.

"There are others." She knew he was complaining because she'd left on his sweater. She closed her fingers around a handful of the wool. "I'll wash this and your long johns in the morning."

He grunted and looked away. Another period of silence passed. He moved only to feed the fire. She moved only to turn an unread page.

Then his rough voice jagged into her again. "I can't believe you sent me for books and tapes. "You'll need more than one change of clothes."

"There were two in the duffel."

"That's not enough if you're stuck here a while."

"You have a washer. I'll do fine. Besides, I have boots in the duffel. I can always go back to the car—"

"*Boots?* Why in the hell didn't you put them on the other night?"

She drew her elbows in tighter. Strangely, this kind of criticism had been less hurtful coming from Richard. "I didn't think the mud would be so bad."

"You didn't think period. Your car's stuck in pretty good. That took some doing."

"I'm not an expert—with cars *or* mud," she argued, but she was shaking inside. She had no idea why he was harping at her this way. "I was only trying to get out—"

"By grinding the tires in deeper?"

"I was trying my best!"

Again he grunted. Again he looked away. Tension made the air nearly as heavy as her heart.

"You didn't even lock the damn car!" he roared a short time later. "With your purse lying there, and all your supposed worldly possessions, you left the thing open!"

"I was too upset to think about that."

"And you're supposed to be a New Yorker?"

She slammed her book shut. "I've never *had* a car before. What is the *problem,* Garrick? You said yourself that no one moves in this kind of weather. Even if someone could, who in his right mind would be going to a burned out cabin? My things were safe, and if they weren't, they're only *things.*"

He snorted. "You'd probably *give* the rest away, now that you've got your precious books and your tapes and your wok—"

"Damn it, Garrick!" she cried, sliding forward on the sofa. "Why are you doing this to me? I don't tell you how to live, do I? If my books mean more to me than clothes, that's *my* choice." Tears sparkled on her lids but she refused to let them fall. "I may not be like other women in that sense, but it's the way I am. Will it really hurt you if I alternate between two outfits? If I'm clean and I don't smell, why should you be concerned? Am I that awful to look at that I need all kinds of fancy things to make my presence bearable?"

She was on her feet, looking at him with hurt-filled eyes. "You don't want me here. I know that, and because of it, I don't want to be here, either. I never asked to be marooned with you. If I'd known what Victoria was planning, I'd never have left New York!" She was breathing hard, trying to control her temper, but without success. "I'm as independent as you are, and I prize that independence. I've earned it. Do you think it's easy for me to be stuck in an isolated cabin with a sharp-tongued, self-indulgent recluse? Well, it isn't! I took enough abuse from my husband. I don't have to take it from you!"

She started to move away, but turned back as quickly. "And since we've taken off the gloves, let me tell you something else. You have the manners of a *boor!* I didn't have to cook dinner tonight. You've made it clear that you're more than happy doing it. But I wanted to do something for *you,* for a change. I wanted to please you. I wanted to show you that I'm not a wimpy female who needs to be waited on. And what did I get for it? Out-and-out rudeness. You took your sweet time deciding whether you'd privilege me with your company at the table. Then after you shoveled food in your mouth, you stormed off as though I'd committed some unpardonable sin. What did I *do?* Can't you at least tell me that? Or is it beyond your capability to share your thoughts once in a while?"

Through her entire tirade, he didn't move a muscle. Throwing her hands up in a gesture of futility, she turned away. Yanking a nightshirt from the duffel she'd stowed under the bed, she fled to the bathroom. A minute later she was out again, throwing her clothes down on top of the duffel, plopping down on the edge of the bed.

Her breath was ragged and her fingers dug into the quilt with fearsome strength. She was angry. She was hurt. But mostly she was dismayed, because she'd taken both her anger and her hurt out on Garrick. It wasn't like her to do that to anyone. She was normally the most composed of women. Yet she'd disintegrated before Garrick. Garrick. After last night.

She didn't see or hear him until he was standing directly before her. Her eyes focused on his legs. She couldn't look up. She didn't know what to say.

Very slowly, he lowered himself to his haunches. She bowed her head even more, but he raised it with a finger beneath her chin. A gentle finger. Her gaze crept upward.

His eyes held the words of apology that his lips wouldn't form, and that gentle finger became five, touching her cheek with soulful hesitance. Callused fingertips moved falteringly, exploring her cheek, her cheekbone, the straight slope of her nose, her lips.

Her breath caught in her throat, because all the while he was touching her, his eyes were speaking, and the words were so sad and humble and heartfelt that she wanted to cry.

He leaned forward, then hesitated.

She touched her fingertips to the thick brush of his beard in encouragement.

This time when he leaned forward he didn't falter, and the words he spoke so silently were the most meaningful of all.

5

Garrick kissed her. It was the first time their lips had touched, and it wasn't so much the touching itself as its manner that shook Leah to the core. His mouth was artful, capturing hers with a gentleness that spoke of caring, a sweetness that spoke of a deep inner need. He brushed his lips back and forth across her softening flesh, then drew back to look at her again.

His eyes caressed each of her features. Setting her glasses aside, he kissed her eyes, the bridge of her nose, her cheekbone, her temple. By the time he returned to her mouth, her lips were parted. She tipped her head to perfect the fit, welcoming him with rapidly flaring desire.

His enthusiasm matched hers. Oh, he'd fought it. All day and all evening he'd been telling himself that he didn't want this or need it, that it would cause more trouble than it was worth. He'd been telling himself that he had the self-control to resist any and all urgings of the flesh. But then Leah had blown up. She'd given him a piece of her mind, and she'd been right in what she'd said. He'd seen and felt her hurt, and he'd known that urgings of the flesh were but a small part of the attraction he felt for her.

He couldn't fight it any longer, because just as his new life was built on control, it was built on honesty. What he felt for Leah, what he needed from her and with her was too raw, too beautiful to be sullied by ugly behavior or lack of communication. He'd talk. He'd tell her about himself. For now, though, he needed to speak with his body.

Calling on everything he'd ever learned about pleasing a woman, he set to pleasing Leah. His mouth was never still, never rough or forceful, demanding only in the most subtle of ways. He stroked her lips, loved them with his own and with his tongue, worshiped the small teeth that lay behind, then the deeper, warmer, moister recesses that beckoned.

There was nothing calculated in what he did. He might have learned and perfected the technique from and on other women, but what he felt as he pleasured Leah came straight from the heart. And he was pleasuring himself, as well, discovering a goodness he'd never known, realizing yet again that what he'd once thought of as purely physical was emotionally uplifting with Leah. In that sense, he was experiencing a rebirth. His past took on meaning, for it was the groundwork from which he could love Leah completely.

She felt it. She felt the wealth of feeling behind the mouth that revered hers, the tongue that flowed around and against hers, the hands that sifted through her hair with such tenderness. She felt things new and different, things that arrowed into her heart and made her tremble.

"Garrick?" she breathed when his lips left hers for a minute.

"Shhhhh—"

"I'm sorry for yelling—"

He was cupping her head, his breath whispering over her. "We'll talk later. I need you too much now." He kissed her once more, lingeringly, then released her to whip his sweatshirt over his head.

Her palms were on him even before the sweatshirt hit the floor. Palms open, fingers splayed, she ran her hands over his chest, covering every inch in greedy possession. He was warm and firm. A fine mat of hair, its tawny hue made golden by the residual light of the fire, wove a manly pattern over his flesh. She explored the broader patch above his breasts and traced its narrowing to his waist, then dragged her hands upward again until they spanned dual swells of muscle and small, tight nipples rasped against her palms.

The breath he expelled was a shuddering one. He had his eyes closed and his head thrown back. His long fingers closed around her wrists, not to stop her voyage but simply because he needed to hold her, to know that he wasn't imagining her touch. His insides were hot; shafts of fire were shooting toward his loins, and a sheen of perspiration had broken out on his skin, adding to the sensual slide of her hands.

When she rounded his shoulders and began to stroke his back in those same, broad sweeps of discovery, he shakily released the buttons of her nightshirt and pushed the soft fabric down her arms. For a minute he could do nothing but look; the perfection before him all but stopped his breathing. Her breasts were round and full, their tips gilded by the firelight. He touched one. Her nipple was already hard, but grew even more so. Sucking in a breath at the sweet pain, Leah closed her fingers on the smooth flesh at his sides and clung for dear life.

His eyes locked with hers, finding a desire there that was echoed in the shallowness of her breathing. "I want to touch you, Leah. I need to. I need to touch and to taste."

She gave a convulsive swallow, then whispered, "Please!"

Unable to help himself, he smiled. She was so adorable, so sexy, so guileless when it came to this. He had to kiss her again, and he did, and while his lips held hers, he touched her breasts. She jerked at the sudden charge of sensation, but he gentled her with his mouth, and his work-roughened hands circled her, covered her, lifted her with care. She never quite got used to his touch, because each time he moved his palm or finger, new currents of awareness sizzled through her. When the pads of his thumbs scored her nipples, soft sounds of arousal came from deep in her throat, and when forefingers joined thumbs in an erotic rolling, a snowballing need had her squirming restlessly.

Her hands moved with desperation to the waistband of his cords. His met them there, unsnapping and unzipping, before leaving her to her own devices. He wanted to touch her more, this time her knees, which were widespread, allowing him to kneel between them, then her thighs, which were soft and smooth and quivering. When her hands slipped beneath the band of his shorts in search of the point of greatest heat, his surged higher, similarly seeking and finding the heart of her sex.

Leah's head fell forward, mouth open, teeth braced on his shoulder. Her hands surrounded him. They measured his length and width, weighed the heaviness beneath. They caressed satin over steel and were rewarded when he strained harder against her palms. But her mind was only half there, because Garrick had opened her and begun to do such intimately arousing things to her that she could barely breathe, much less think.

She'd never thought of herself as lacking control where sex was concerned, but she'd never been half as hot as she was now. She felt herself floating, rising, and her attempts to rein in were futile. Sandwiching the power of his virility between them, her hands went still.

"Garrick…oh…oh." She sucked in a breath, let it out in a tremulous whisper. "Please…I need…wait."

But just then he took her nipple into his mouth, and it was too late. The brush of his mustache and beard and his gentle sucking snapped the fine thread from which she'd been hanging. Her thighs closed on his hands as her insides exploded, and she could only gasp against his shoulder while she rode out a storm of endless spasms. When they subsided at last, she rolled her face to the crook of his neck.

"I'm sorry…I couldn't hold back…"

Framing her face, he raised it and kissed her. His lips shifted and angled and sucked, never once leaving hers as he bore her gently back on the bed. His hands tugged the nightshirt from her hips, then went to work baring himself. Naked, he lowered his large frame over her.

Leah was ready to take him in, but he had no intention of simply slaking his desire while she lay quiescent and sated. He wanted her hungry again. He wanted her aroused and aching for him, because he knew that if it was so, his own fulfillment would be all the richer.

So he began to touch her anew. Her breasts, her belly, that ultrasensitive spot between her legs—he stimulated and teased, using hands, lips and tongue. And he was doing just fine until she became active herself, finding the places that set him to shaking, stroking them, tormenting them with fingers that were innocent and eager to please.

And Garrick was pleased, though the word seemed a paltry one to describe his feelings. He'd never felt so valued—not just needed, *valued*. Beneath Leah's hands and lips and the sweet waft of her breath, he felt cherished, special and unique. He felt as though she couldn't be doing this with any other man but him.

At that moment, he knew the future would have to take care of itself. He needed her now and for however long she chose to stay with him. If, at the end of that time, he was alone, he knew that he'd have experienced something most men never even approach. He'd have memories of something rare and wonderful, and he'd be a stronger man for it.

Writhing gently beneath him, Leah urged him to her. He grasped her hands, intertwined his fingers with hers and pinned them to the quilt by her shoulders. Poised above her, he watched her face as slowly, slowly he entered her.

Her eyes fell shut and a tiny smile of bliss curved her lips. Then, with a sigh, she lifted her legs and wrapped them tightly around him. "Don't move," she whispered, still smiling in that catlike way that gave him a thrill. "You feel...I feel so...good...full."

"Leah?" he whispered.

Slowly her eyes opened. They were filled with the same love that filled his heart. He knew it was absurd. He and Leah had known each other for only two days, and those under unusual conditions. They hadn't talked much, hadn't shared thoughts of the past or the future, much less the present, but he *did* love her. He'd never felt anything like it before—the driving desire to please a woman, to make her happy in the broadest sense— but he felt that way toward Leah. He felt that he'd will- ingly sacrifice his quiet to hear her music, his steak and potatoes to eat her Chinese food, his normal efficiency to take her floundering in the mud. He knew that if she asked him to withdraw from her just then, he'd forgo a climax and still feel complete.

She didn't ask him anything of the sort, though. Rather, she began to move her hips and her inner mus- cles, holding him ever more tightly, taking his breath away. Lifting her head from the pillow, she sought his lips, and he lost track of everything but the intense plea- sure of stroking her tongue and drawing it into his mouth. Bowing his back, he withdrew, then thrust for- ward, withdrew, then thrust forward. With each thrust he went deeper. With each withdrawal, he returned hot- ter. Finally, with a surge that touched her womb, he stiffened and held, erupting into a release so powerful that he thought he'd die, so glorious that he would have welcomed it.

Only when awareness returned did he realize that Leah, too, was vibrating in the aftermath of climax. Her cheek was pressed to their intertwined hands. Her eyes were shut tightly. Her lips were parted to allow for the soft panting that was sweet music to his ears. He was glad then that he hadn't died, for there was more to come, so much more.

Very gently he slid from her, but before she could protest, he'd nestled her snugly into the crook of his shoulder. One of his arms encircled her back, the other grasped her thigh and drew it over his. His fingers remained in a warm clasp around her knee.

Eyes closed, Leah sighed in contentment. She rubbed her nose against Garrick's chest, inhaling the scent of man and musk and sex that would have been arousing had not she been so thoroughly sated.

"Ahhh, Garrick," she whispered. "So nice…"

"It is, isn't it?" he responded as softly. In the past he would have been reaching for a cigarette. Putting distance between himself and the body next to him. Biding the few obligatory minutes before he could clear whatever woman he was with from his bed. Now, though, the only thing he wanted to do was lie holding Leah. And talk.

"You're spectacular," she said. "Maybe I should yell at you more."

That drew a lazy chuckle from his throat. "Maybe you should. It brings me to my senses."

"I'm not usually the yelling type."

"I'm not usually the brooding type."

"What brought it on?"

He cuffed his chin against the top of her head, knowing that his beard would cushion the gentle blow. "You."

"Is it that difficult having me here?"

"Just the opposite. I like having you here."

"Then why—"

"I like it too much. I thought I had my life all worked out. Then you pop in and upset the apple cart."

"Oh." She took a quick breath. "I know what you mean."

"You do?"

"Mmm. I haven't minded living alone—living without a man. I thought it was the safest thing."

"Did your marriage hurt you that much?"

"Yes."

"You said he abused you. Was it physical?"

"He never beat me. It was more an emotional thing."

"Tell me about him. What was he like?"

Leah thought for a minute, seeking to express her feelings with a minimum of bitterness. "He was good-looking and charming. He could sell an icebox to an Eskimo."

"He was a salesman?"

"Indirectly. He was—is—a top executive in an ad agency. If you want to know what charisma is, you don't have to look farther than Richard. People flock to him. He attracts clients like flies. Lord only knows why he married me."

Garrick gave her a sharp squeeze, but she went on.

"I'm serious. I guess it was the stage he was at when we met. He was just getting started. He needed a wife who looked relatively sophisticated, and when I try, I suppose I do look that. He needed someone who knew the ins and outs of New York, and since I'd lived there all my life, I guess I qualified on that score, too. He needed someone he could manipulate, and I fit the bill."

"You don't strike *me* as being terribly manipulatable," Garrick said with feeling.

She laughed. "How can you say that after what Victoria did?"

"That may be the one exception, and since we were both patsies, we won't count it."

"Well, Richard was able to manipulate me. I wanted to please him. I wanted to make the marriage work."

"Why didn't it?"

"Oh, lots of reasons. Mainly because I couldn't be what Richard wanted."

"Couldn't?"

"That, and wouldn't. I got tired of being told when to be where wearing what. I got tired of feeling that regardless how hard I tried, I didn't measure up."

"What did the guy want?" Garrick barked. The sound reverberated in his chest beneath Leah's ear. Knowing that he was on her side, she didn't mind his anger.

"Perfection."

"None of us is perfect."

"Tell that to Richard."

"Thanks, but I'll pass. He sounds like the kind of guy I avoid."

"You're very wise."

"Either that, or very weak. I haven't quite decided which yet."

Leah shifted, turning her head so that she looked up at him. "You, weak? I don't believe that for a minute. Look at the way you live. It takes strength to do what you do."

"Physical strength, yes."

"No, psychological. To live alone on a mountainside, to be comfortable enough with yourself to live alone— many people can't do that."

It was the perfect opening. He knew he should say something about himself and his past, but the words wouldn't come. He wanted Leah's respect. He feared he'd risk it if she knew where he'd been. "I'm not sure I've done it so well, judging from the way I've latched on to you." Hauling her higher on his chest, he gave her a fierce kiss. But the fierceness mellowed quickly. "You taste so good, Leah," he whispered hoarsely. "You *feel* so good." His hands had begun to glide up and down her body. "You feel so good on top of me."

That was precisely where she was. Her breasts were pillowed by the soft furring of his chest hair. Her thighs, straddling his, knew their sinewed strength. He felt so good beneath her that her body began a slow rocking while her mouth inched over his nose, his cheek and down to the warm, bare skin below his beard.

"You smell good," she whispered against his throat.

Garrick grinned in pure delight. He felt redeemed, almost defiant. He smelled earthy, but Leah liked it. So there, L.A.! Take your Brut and stuff it!

"Garrick?" Her voice was muffled against his chest.

"What is it, love?"

She kept her face buried. "I want you again."

He laughed in continued delight.

"What's so funny?"

"You. You're wonderful."

"Does that mean you want me, too?"

He arched his hips against hers. "What do you think?"

"I think yes, but maybe you think I'm only after your body."

He didn't laugh this time. Instead his long fingers

caged her head and gently raised it. His expression was soft and filled with wonder. "What I think is that I'm the luckiest man alive." He didn't say anything else, because his mouth covered hers. His hands spread over her hips, lifting, lowering, until she was fully impaled.

Leah had seldom been in the dominant position, but her desire more than compensated for her lack of experience. He guided her at first, moving her up and down in slow, sure strokes, but then he began caressing her breasts and she let instinct be her guide. She heard the quickening of his breathing and increased rhythm. She felt him lower his head and craned upward so he could reach her breasts with his lips. She sensed when he approached his climax and ground herself more tightly against him. And when he cried out in release, she was with him all the way.

When her heartbeat finally slowed she thought she'd be exhausted, but she wasn't. Her body was sated, but her mind had only begun to hunger. She wanted to talk. It was as though a dam had burst, years of holding in thoughts and questions given way now to a steady flow. She was fearing that Garrick would rather sleep, when his voice drifted over her brow.

"I've never had a woman here before."

They'd slipped between the sheets and were snuggled warmly and closely. "I know," she breathed against his chest.

"I've never had much of anyone here before. Another trapper will stop by once in a while. And buyers come for my furs."

"Is that only in the winter?"

"Pretty much so. I can't trap the good stuff after the middle of January."

"The good stuff—fisher, fox and raccoon?"

"Um-hmm."

"Why not after the middle of January?"

"That's the law, and it makes sense. The furs are thickest in winter, and prime fur draws the best price. But that's secondary to the concept of wildlife management."

"Explain."

"The theory is that hunting and trapping shouldn't be done to exploit the wildlife population, but to control it. Raccoon threaten local cornfields. Beaver threaten the free flow of streams."

"You don't have to justify what you do."

"But it's all part of the explanation. Trapping isn't a free-for-all. At the beginning of each season, the Fish and Game Department issues strict guidelines, in some cases limiting the catch of certain species. For example, I can take only three fisher a year. With roughly eight hundred trappers in the state, three fisher per trapper, the number adds up. If limits aren't set, the population will be endangered."

"How are limits set?"

"The department decides based on information it gets from trappers the previous year. Every catch I make has to be tagged. I tell the department where and when I made the catch, what condition the animal was in and what I observed about the overall population while I was running my trapline."

"Then the limits vary by year?"

"Theoretically, yes. But in the past few years the various populations have been stable, which means that the department has been doing its job right. Once in a while there's politicking involved. For example, fisher feed on turkeys and rabbits. The turkey and rabbit hunters lobby for a higher take of fisher, so that there will be more turkeys and rabbits left for them to hunt."

"Do they win?"

"No. At one point, in the early thirties, fisher were hunted nearly to extinction. The department is very protective of them now."

"But why the January deadline?"

"Because come February, the mating season begins. Trapping after that would be a double hazard to the population."

"Then you trap only three months a year?"

"I can take beaver through the end of March and coyote whenever I want. But the first I use mainly for bait, and the second don't interest me other than to keep them away from my traps. They'll eat the best of my catch if I let them. And they're smart, coyotes are. Trap a coyote in one place, and the rest don't go near that spot again."

Leah loved hearing him talk, not only for his low, husky voice, almost a murmur as they lay twined together, but for his knowledge, as well. "It must be an art—successful trapping."

"Part art, part science. It's hard work, even for those few short months."

"A little more complicated than sticking a spigot in a tree, hmm?"

He chuckled. "A little. The work starts well before the trapping season opens. I have to get a license, plus written permission from any private landowners whose land I may be crossing. I have to prepare the traps—season new ones, repair and prime old ones. Once the season opens and I've set my traps, I have to run the line every morning."

"Every morning?"

"Early every morning."

"You don't mind that?"

"Nah. I like it." He never used to like getting up. When he'd worked in L.A., he'd hated early morning calls. More often than not he'd been partying late the night before, and particularly in the later years, he'd awoken hung over. There were no parties here, though, and no drinks. He had no trouble waking up. Indeed, he'd discovered that the post-dawn hours were peaceful and productive.

"Why early in the morning?"

"Because most of the furbearers are nocturnal, which means that they'll be out foraging, hence caught at night. I want to collect them as soon as possible after they step into the trap."

"Why?"

He laughed. It occurred to him that he'd laughed more in the past few hours than he had in weeks.

"What's so funny?"

He hugged her closer. "You. Your curiosity. It never quits."

"But it's interesting, what you do. Do you mind my questions?"

"No. I don't mind your questions." And he meant it, which surprised him almost as much as the sound of his own repeated laughter. The past four years of his life had been dominated by silence. He'd needed it at first, because he hadn't been fit to carry on any conversation, much less one with a woman. He'd spoken only when necessary, and then with locals who'd been blessedly laconic. Even the old man who'd taught him to trap had been a miser where words were concerned, and that had suited Garrick just fine. He welcomed words that held real meaning, rather than shallow platitudes. He'd had his fill of the latter—sweet talk meant to impress, crude talk meant to hurt, idle talk meant to pass the time, patronizing talk meant to buy or win.

He'd never had the kind of gentle, innocently genuine talk that he now shared with Leah, and he wasn't sure he'd ever get his fill. Unusual as it was to discuss trapping in the dark after lovemaking, he was enjoying it.

"Why do I want to collect my catch as soon as possible? Because if I wait, the fox may close in or the fur may be otherwise damaged. Once I've made the catch, I try to concentrate on the art of preparing the fur."

"There's an art to it?"

"Definitely. For example, when it comes to fleshing…" He hesitated. "You don't need to hear this."

"Okay," she said so quickly that he chuckled again, but she was immediately off on a related tangent. "So the trapping season is pretty short. What do you do during the rest of the year?"

"Read. Whittle. Go birding in the woods. Grow vegetables."

She popped up over him. "Vegetables? Where?"

"Out back."

"What's out back? There aren't any windows on that wall so I haven't been able to see."

He stroked her cheek with a lazy thumb. "There's a

clearing. It's small, but it gets enough sun in the summer months to grow what I need."

"You eat it all?"

"Not all. You can only consume so much lettuce."

"Lettuce. What else?"

"Tomatoes, carrots, zucchini, peas, green beans. I freeze a lot of stuff for the winter months. Whatever is left over, I give away. Or trade. The maple syrup we had with the pancakes came that way."

"Not bad," she said. Her hands were splayed over his chest. Dipping her head, she dropped an impulsive kiss on the hollow of his throat. "Actually, I'm in awe. I have a brown thumb. Plants die on me right and left. I finally gave up trying to grow them, which I suppose is just as well. If I'd been attached to a plant and then had to give it away when I packed up to come here—"

"You could have brought it."

"It's a good thing I didn't. I mean, here I am with most of my stuff still in the car in the cold. Victoria's place is worthless, and I have no idea where I'll be going—"

Garrick cut off the flow of her words by flipping her onto her back and sealing her mouth with his. He didn't want her to talk about going anywhere. He didn't want her to *think* about going anywhere. He wanted her to love him again.

Leah needed little urging. The weight of his body covering her, pressing her to the mattress, branding her with blatant masculinity was enough to spark fires that she'd thought long since banked. They kissed again and again. They began to touch and explore with even greater boldness than before. Lines and curves that should have been familiar by now took on newness from different angles, heightening the fever that rose between them until, once again, they came together in the ultimate stroke of passion.

This time, when it was over and they'd fallen languidly into each other's arms, they lay quietly.

After a bit Leah whispered, "Garrick?"

"Hmm?"

"I've never done this before."

"Hmm?"

"Three times in one night. I never thought I had it in me. I never wanted to…more than once."

"Know something?" he returned in the same whisper. "Me, neither."

"Really?"

"Really." Strange, but he was proud to say it. How often he'd lied in the past, how many times he'd bragged about nonstop bouts of sex. He'd had an image to uphold, but it had been an empty one. If a woman had asked for more, he'd always had a ready answer; either she'd worn him out, or the woman the night before had worn him out, or he had an early call in the morning. The fact was that once his initial lust had been fed he'd lost interest.

But it wasn't lust he felt for Leah. Well, maybe a little, but there was love in it, too, and that made all the difference.

"How long have you been here, Garrick?"

"Four years."

"And you went places when you felt the need…the urge to…"

"I haven't felt it much, but there were women I could see."

"Were they nice?"

"They were okay."

"Do you still see any of them?"

"No. One-night stands were about all I could handle."

"Why?"

Again she'd given him an opening. He could easily explain that he'd been going through a rough time, finding himself, but then she'd ask more questions, and he didn't want to have to answer them. Not tonight. So he gave an answer that was honest, if simplified. "None of them made me want anything more."

"Oh."

"What does that mean—oh?"

"Are you gonna kick me out tomorrow?"

"I can't. Remember, the mud?"

She scraped the nail of her big toe against his shin. "If it weren't for the mud, would you kick me out?"

"We've already had more than a one-night stand."

"You're not answering my question."

"How can I kick you out? You have nowhere to go."

"Garrick…"

His elbow tightened around her neck. "No, Leah, I would not kick you out. I will not kick you out. I like having you here. You can stay as long as you want."

"Because I'm good in bed?"

"Yes."

"Garrick!"

"Because I like being *with* you. How's that?"

"Better."

"You want more?"

"Yes."

"Because you do things for my sweater that I never did."

"I thought you wanted it back."

"I want you to keep it. Wear it."

"Okay."

"And you can cook if you want."

"But you hate Chinese food."

"I didn't hate what you made tonight. I was just being difficult." He paused, then ventured more cautiously. "Do you do anything besides Chinese?"

"I've taken courses in French cooking. And Indian. I doubt you have the ingredients for either of those."

"Do you always cook foreign for yourself in New York?"

"Oh, no."

"What do you normally eat?"

"When I'm not pigging out with Victoria?"

"Come to think of it, you do eat a lot. How do you stay so thin?"

"Lean Cuisines."

"Excuse me?"

"Lean Cuisines. They're frozen. I heat them in the microwave."

"You eat *frozen dinners?*"

"Sure. They're good. A little too much sodium, but otherwise they provide a balanced meal."

"Oh. If you say so."

She yawned. "I do."

"Tired?"

"A little. What time is it?"

"I don't know. I don't have a watch."

She held her wrist before his nose. "I don't have my glasses. What time does it say?"

"Twenty past a freckle."

"Oh." She dropped her hand to his chest. "I left my watch in the bathroom."

"That's okay. The fire's gone out, so I wouldn't have been able to read it anyway."

"It has a luminous dial."

"You come prepared."

"Usually." She burrowed closer, stifling another yawn. "I don't want to go to sleep. I like talking with you."

"Me, too."

"Will we talk more in the morning, or are you going to go mute on me with the break of day?"

He chuckled. "We'll talk more."

"Promise?"

"Scout's honor."

"Were you a Scout?"

"Once upon a time."

"I want to hear about it," she murmured, but she was fading fast.

"You will."

"Garrick?"

"Mmm?"

It was a while before she answered and then her words were slurred. "How old are you?"

"Forty." He waited for her to say something more. When she didn't, he whispered her name. She didn't answer. Smiling, he pressed a soft kiss to her rumpled bangs.

6

When Leah awoke the next morning, Garrick was beside her. He was sprawled on his stomach, his head facing away, but one of his ankles was hooked around hers in a warm reminder of the events of the night before. Heart swelling with happiness, she took a deep breath and stretched. Then she rolled against him, slipped a slender arm over his waist and sighed contentedly.

Weak slivers of light filtered through the shutters, dimly illuminating the room. It was still raining, she knew, but the patter on the roof had eased to a gentle tap, and anyway, she didn't care what the weather was. Garrick had said she could stay as long as she wanted. She wasn't going to think about leaving.

When the body against her shifted, she slid her hand forward, up over his middle to his chest. His own covered it, and then he was turning to look at her.

It was the very first time in his life that Garrick had awoken pleased to find a woman in his bed. He smiled. "Hi."

Oh, how she loved his voice, even that lone word, working like fine sandpaper to make her tingle. "Hi."

"How did you sleep?"

"Like a baby."

"You don't look like a baby." His gaze was roaming her face, taking in the luster of mussed hair on her forehead, the luminous gray of her eyes, the softness of lips that had been well kissed not so very long ago. "You look sexy."

She blushed. "So do you."

His eyes skimmed lower, over her neck to her breasts. "I've never seen you in daylight," he said softly.

"You have."

"Not nude." Very gently he eased back the covers, allowing himself a full view of her body. His gaze touched her waist, the visible line of her pelvis and the length of her legs before returning to linger on the shadowed apex of her thighs. "You're lovely."

Leah was trembling, but not only because of the way he was looking and the sensual sound of his voice. When he'd pulled back the covers he'd bared himself, as well, and what she saw was breathtaking. With his tapering torso, his lean hips and tightly muscled legs, he was a great subject for a sculptor. But it was his sex that held her spellbound, for it was perfectly formed, incredibly full and heavy.

"I do want you," he whispered. "I think I've been like this all night, dreaming of you."

"You don't have to dream," she breathed. "I'm here."

"So hard to believe…" Shifting so that he crouched over her, he let his hands drift over each part of her in turn. When he reached her belly, he sat back on his haunches, then watched his fingers lower to brush the dark tangle of curls. He stroked her lightly, but even that light touch spread heat like wildfire through her veins.

"Garrick…"

"Warm and beautiful."

"I need you…"

His eyes met hers, and there was an intensity in them that held more than one form of passion. "I want you, too. I want that more than anything."

When she reached for him, he lifted her and crushed her close. They held each other that way for a long time, bodies flush, limbs faintly quivering. Oddly, the desire to make love passed, replaced by the gratification of simply being together. At that moment it seemed much more precious than anything else in the world.

Garrick's arms were the first to slacken. "I need a shower," he said in a voice lingering with emotion. "Want to share?"

"I've never taken a shower with a man before."

"Never?"

"Never."

"Are you game?"

"If you are. It's a large shower."

"I'm a large man."

"Which means—"

"We'll be close."

"I'd like that."

"Me, too." Scooping her into his arms, he rolled to the edge of the bed. "Come on."

"I can walk."

"The floor's cold."

"You're walking."

"Would you rather switch places?"

"You're too heavy."

"Then hush."

When he reached the bathroom, he lowered her feet to the floor, turned to start the water, then knelt before her and very gently removed the bandage from her leg. She'd given up on gauze and adhesive the day before in favor of a Band-Aid, and the only discomfort she still felt was from the black-and-blue area surrounding the cut.

"Looks okay," he decided, then slid his gaze leisurely up her body. "I like the rest better, though."

She finger-combed his hair back from his forehead. "I'm glad."

After pressing a soft kiss on her navel, he stood and led her into the shower. They soaped themselves and then, for the hell of it, each other. And it *was* hell in some ways, because the glide of suds beneath palms over various bodily areas was erotic, but they didn't want to make love. Resisting the temptation was in part a game, in part a way of saying that there was more to their relationship than sex.

Touching was totally acceptable, and they did it constantly. It astounded Leah that two people who'd been alone for so long could adapt so easily to such closeness. Or maybe it was *because* they'd been alone that they were greedy. Either way, they never strayed far from each other. They watched each other dress—chipping in to help here and there with a button or a sock. Likewise, they chipped in making breakfast, then ate with their legs entwined under the table.

And they talked—constantly and about anything that came to mind.

"I love your hair," Garrick said. He'd settled her onto his lap when she'd come around to clear his plate. "Have you always worn it this way?"

"No. I had it cut the day my divorce became final."

"Celebrating?"

"Declaring my independence. When I was little I always wore my hair long. My mother loved combing it and curling it and tying it up with ribbons. Richard liked it long, too. It was part of the image. He thought long hair was alluring. Y'know," she drawled, "waving tresses sweeping over sequined shoulders." Her voice returned to its normal timbre. "Sometimes he'd have me wear it up, sometimes hitched back with a fancy comb. I used to have to spend hours getting it to look just right. I hated it."

"So you cut it."

"Yup."

He stroked the silky strands. "It's so pretty this way."

"It's easy."

"Then pretty *and* easy." He scalloped a gentle thumb through her bangs. "Did you like going out?"

"Where?"

"To parties, restaurants."

"With Richard? No. And I still don't like parties, but maybe that's because I feel awkward."

"Why would you feel awkward?" he asked in the same gravelly voice she found so soothing. It eased her over the embarrassment of expressing particular thoughts.

"I've never been a social butterfly. I was shy."

"Shy? Really?"

Smiling, she wrapped her arms around his neck and nuzzled his hair. "Really."

"Why shy?"

Sitting back, she shrugged. "I don't know. I was an

English major, a bookworm, an…intellectual. I suppose one of the things that snowed me about Richard was that he was good with people in a way I wasn't. I could go places with him and be part of the crowd in a way I'd never been."

"Did you like that?"

"I thought I would, and I did at first. Then I realized that I wasn't really part of the crowd. *He* was, but I wasn't. I was just along for the ride, but the ride wasn't fun. The people were boring. I didn't have much to say to them. Richard was always after me to be more pleasant, and I could be charming when I tried, but under the circumstances, I hated it. The whole thing came to be uncomfortable."

He eased her to her feet and reached for the plates. "I can understand that."

Leah didn't have to ask him if he agreed, because she knew he did. If he liked crowds and parties and small talk, he'd never have chosen to live alone in the woods. As they began to load the dishwasher, it occurred to her to ask why he'd chosen to live this way. Instead she asked, "Why are you studying Latin?"

"Because it's interesting. So many of our words have Latin derivatives."

"You didn't study it as a kid?"

"Nope. I studied Spanish. My mom was a Spanish professor."

"No kidding!"

"No kidding." The way he said it—part drawl, part resignation—suggested more to the story. This particular chapter didn't threaten Leah.

"Oh-oh. It wasn't great?"

"She was very involved in her work. When she wasn't teaching, she was traveling to one Spanish-speaking area or another, and when she wasn't doing that, she was entertaining students at our house."

"You didn't like that?"

"I would have liked a little of her attention myself."

"What about your father? What did he do?"

"He was a gastroenterologist."

"And very busy."

"Uh-huh."

"You were alone a lot."

"Uh-huh."

"Do you have any brothers or sisters?"

He shook his head and handed her the pan he'd just washed. "How about you?"

"I was an only, too. But my parents doted on me. Isn't it strange that we should have had such different experiences? Perhaps if we'd been able to put our four parents in a barrel and shake them up, we'd each have had a little more of what we needed."

He chuckled, but it was a sad sound. "If only."

When they finished cleaning the kitchen, Garrick made a fire, then sat on the floor with his back against the sofa and pulled Leah between his legs. She nestled into the haven, crossing her arms over those stronger, more manly ones that wound around her middle.

"Have you always worn glasses?" he asked, his breath warm by her ear.

"From the time I was twelve. I wore contacts for Richard, but I never really liked them."

"Why not?"

"It was a pain—putting them in every morning, taking them out and cleaning them every night, enzyming them once a week. Besides, nearsightedness is *me*. On principle alone, I don't see why I should have to hide it."

"You look adorable with glasses."

Smiling, she offered a soft, "Thank you." Her smile lingered for a long time. "This is…so…nice," she whispered at last. "I feel so peaceful." She tipped her head back to see his face. "Is that what you feel living up here?"

"More so since you've come."

"But before. Is it the peace that appeals to you?"

"It's lots of things. Peace, yes. Lack of hassle. I work hard enough, but at my own speed."

Implicit was the suggestion that he'd known something very different four years before. Again she had an opportunity to probe that past. Again she let it slide. Returning her gaze to the fire, she asked, "Do you ever get bored?"

"No. There's always something to do."

"When did you learn to whittle?"

"Soon after I came."

"Did the trapper teach you?"

"I taught myself. One good instruction book, and I was on my way."

"What do you make?"

"Whatever strikes me. Mostly carvings of animals I see in the woods."

"I don't see any here. Don't you keep them?"

"Some." They were out in the shed, which he'd come to think of as a sort of studio-gallery. "I give some away. I sell some."

"Do you?" she asked, grinning widely. "You must be good."

"Yes to the first, I don't know to the second."

"If people buy them…" she said in a tone that made her point. "Have you always been artistic?" Images of the artists Richard employed crossed her mind. There was a high burnout rate in the advertising world. Perhaps that was what had happened to Garrick.

But he was shaking his head, his chin ruffling her hair. "Not particularly. It was only after I came here that I found I liked working with my hands."

"You're very good with your hands," she teased, and was rewarded with a tickle. "Anyway, I think it's great. Do you have to use special kinds of wood when you whittle?"

"Soft wood is best—like white pine. It has few knots and very little grain. I use harder wood—birch or maple—when I carve chessmen."

"You make *chess* sets?"

He nodded. "Do you play?"

"No, but I've always admired beautiful sets in store windows. More than once, I thought of buying one just to use it for decoration on a coffee table, but somehow that seemed pretentious. I play checkers, though. Have you ever carved a checker set?"

"Not yet, but I can. God, I haven't played checkers since I was a kid!"

"It'd be fun," she mused. "What about knives?"

"I never played with them."

"Whittling. Do you have special knives? The thing you were using the other night looked like a regular old jackknife."

"It was."

Again she tipped back her head, this time looking up at him in surprise. "A regular old jackknife?"

"Carefully sharpened. It has three blades. I use the largest for rough cutting and the two smaller ones for close work."

She was staring at him, fascinated. "You have beautiful eyes. I don't think I've ever seen hazel shot with silver like that."

The suddenness of the comment took Garrick off guard. It was the type of observation he was used to from his past, yet now it was different. As it sank in, he felt a warming all over. He liked it when Leah complimented him, didn't even mind that she'd been distracted from what he'd been saying. Strange that she didn't recognize him…

"Do you ever watch television?" he asked.

"Rarely. Why?"

"I was just wondering…whether you missed it up here."

"No," she answered, turning her head forward, "and I don't miss a phone, either."

"Didn't use it much at home?"

"Yes."

"Then why don't you miss it now?"

"Because in New York it's a necessity. You have to call to find out whether the book you ordered arrived or to make a reservation at a restaurant. You have to call a friend in advance to make a date for lunch. Up here you don't."

"Did you leave many friends in New York?"

"A few. It's only since my divorce that I've been able

to cultivate friendships. Richard wasn't interested in the people I liked."

"Why not?"

"He didn't think they were useful enough."

"Ahh, he's the user type."

"He didn't step on people. He simply avoided those with whom he couldn't clearly identify. He had to feel that there was a purpose in any and every social contact. Getting together with someone simply because you liked him or her didn't qualify as purposeful in Richard's mind."

Garrick was about to say something critical, when he caught himself. He'd been guilty of the same thing once, only it sounded as though Richard had weathered it better. So who was he to throw stones?

Shifting Leah so that she was cradled sideways on his lap, he asked softly, "What are your friends like?"

Arms looped loosely around his neck, she brushed her thumb against his beard. "Victoria you know. Then there's Greta. We met at a cooking class. She has a phenomenal mathematical mind."

"What does she do?"

"She's an accountant."

"Do you see each other often?"

"Once every few weeks."

"What do you do together?"

"Shop."

"*Shop?* That's the last thing I'd expect an accountant to want to do."

"She doesn't want to. She *has* to. She's in a large firm that makes certain demands, one of which is that she look reasonably well put together. Poor Greta is the first to admit she has no taste at all when it comes to clothes. When we go shopping, I help her choose things, soup to nuts." She grinned. "I'm great at spending other people's money."

"That's naughty."

"Not when it's at their own request and for their own good."

"Is Greta pleased with the results?"

"Definitely."

"Then I guess it's okay. Who are some of your other friends?"

"There's Arlen."

"Is that a he or a she?"

"A she. I don't have any male friends. Except you." She plopped a wet kiss on his cheek. "You're a nice man."

"That's what you say now," he teased. "Wait till you know me better." He'd been thinking about cabin fever, about what could happen to two people, however compatible, when they were stuck with each other day after day. He knew it wouldn't bother him; he was used to the mountain, and he loved Leah. But suddenly he wasn't even thinking about whether Leah loved him back. He was thinking about all he hadn't told her about himself. What he'd said had to have been a Freudian slip.

"I am a nice man," he said seriously. "I wasn't always. But those days are done." He took a quick breath. "Tell me about Arlen."

Leah studied his face a minute longer, unaware of the fear in her eyes. *I wasn't always,* he'd said. What had he been before? Oh, Lord, she didn't want anything to pop her bubble of happiness. Not when she'd waited all her life to find it!

"Arlen." She cleared her throat. "Arlen and I met in the waiting room of the dentist's office. Three years ago, actually." They'd both been pregnant at the time. "We struck up a friendship and kept in touch, then started getting together after Richard and I split. She helped me through some rough times."

"The divorce?"

That, too. "Yes."

"Does she work?"

"Like a dog. She has five kids under the age of eight."

"Whew. She isn't a single mother, is she?"

"No, and her husband's as lovely as she is. They live in Port Washington. I've been to their home several times. She barbecues a mean hot dog."

He grinned. "You like hot dogs?"

"Yeah, but y'know which ones I like best?"

"No. Which ones?"

"You'll think I'm crazy."

"Which ones?"

"The ones you buy at the stands on the edge of Central Park. There's something about the atmosphere—"

"Diesel fumes, horse dung and pigeon shit."

She jabbed at his chest with a playful fist. "You're polluting the image! Think gorgeous spring day when the leaves are just coming into bloom, or hot summer day when the park is an oasis in the middle of the city. Brisk fall day when the leaves flutter to the ground. There's something about visiting the park on days like those and eating a hot dog that may very well kill you that's…that's sybaritic."

"Sybaritic?"

"Well, maybe not sybaritic. How about frivolous?"

"I can live with that." He could also come close to duplicating a sybaritic kind of atmosphere for her here on the mountain. "What else do you like about New York?"

"The anonymity. I feel threatened by large groups that know me and expect certain things that I may or may not be able to deliver. I don't like to have to conform to other people's standards."

He knew that what she was voicing related in part to the shyness she'd mentioned, but that it was a legacy of her marriage to Richard, as well. He was also stunned because the threat was one he himself felt.

"I'm a total unknown on the streets of New York," she went on. "I can pick and choose my friends and do my own thing without being censured. I think I'd die in a small suburban community. I don't want to have to keep up with the Joneses."

"If anyone's doing the keeping up, it should be the Joneses with you."

"God forbid. I don't want any *part* of people who compete their way through life."

"Amen," he said softly, then, "What else?"

"What else, what?"

"What else do you like about New York?"

She didn't have to think long. "The cultural opportunities. And the courses. I love taking courses, learning new things. Victoria said that there was an artists' community not far from here where I'd be able to learn to weave."

"I know just the one. You want to weave?"

"The process fascinates me. I'd like to be able to cre-ate my own patterns and make scarves and rugs and beautiful wall hangings." She lowered suddenly sheep-ish eyes to her fingers, which toyed idly with the cables on his sweater. "At least, I'd like to try."

"You'll do it." He'd build her a loom himself. The thought of seeing her working it, of listening to the rhythmic shift of harnesses, filled him with a mellow-ness that spelled home.

Home. Surprising. He hadn't spent much time think-ing of having a home. What he'd known as a child had been far from ideal, and when he'd gone off to put his name up in lights, he hadn't had the time to think of it. His world had been the public eye. His interests had re-volved around things that would make him more fa-mous. A home didn't do those things. A home was personal, private. It was something for a man and his family.

"Garrick?" Leah whispered.

He blinked, only then realizing that his eyes had grown moist.

"What is it?" Her voice was laden with concern, her eyes with fear. During moments like these, when he looked so sad and faraway, she felt her bubble begin to quiver. He had a past, and for whatever his reasons, he wasn't telling her about it. She didn't have the courage to ask.

He forced a tremulous smile, then drew her in and held her close. "I get to dreaming sometimes," he mur-mured into her hair. "It's scary."

"Can you share the dream?"

"Not yet."

"Maybe someday soon?"

"Maybe."

They sat that way for a while, holding each other quietly. When the fire gave a loud crack and hiss, they both looked around, startled.

"Is it trying to tell us something?" Leah whispered.

"Nah. It's just being insolent."

"Maybe we'd better feed it."

"I have a better idea. Why don't we get dressed and go out?"

Her eyes lit up. "Me, too?"

"You, too." He tipped his head. "Going stir-crazy being inside?"

"No. I just don't want you going out alone. I want to be with you."

"God, you have all the right answers," he breathed.

Her voice held a touch of sadness. "No. Not yet. Maybe soon."

So they went out in the rain, which, mercifully, was more like a drizzle. Garrick led her up the mountain, pointing out various signs of wildlife along the way. The going was sloppy, but in broad daylight and with as indulgent a guide as he was, Leah managed remarkably well. She wasn't quite sure how it happened, but the mountain that had seemed so hostile to her once was now, even in the wet mist, a place of fascination. Garrick belonged, and she was his welcome guest; it was almost as though the landscape had accepted her presence.

After they'd returned to the lower altitude, they trekked to Leah's car and came back carrying more of her things, which he enthusiastically made room for in the cabin and helped her stow.

Later in the day, they succumbed to their urges and made long, sweet love before the fire. In its aftermath, wrapped in each other and a quilt, Leah smiled. "I wonder if Victoria has ESP."

"If so, no doubt she's happy."

"Are you?"

"Very."

She tipped up her face and whispered, "I love you, Garrick."

His eyes went soft and moist. Taking a tremulous breath, he tightened his arms around her. "I love you, too. I've never said that to another living soul, but I do love you, Leah. God, do I love you!" His lips took hers with a fierceness that had never been there before, but Leah didn't mind, because she shared the feeling behind them. The love that flooded her was so powerful that it demanded no less ardent a release.

In the days that followed, their love grew even stronger. They spent every minute together, and never once did they tire of each other's company. There was always something to say, usually in soft, intimate tones, but there were times when they were silent, communicating simply with a look, a touch or a smile.

Garrick showed her his shed and the whittled figures that sat on a long shelf. Not only did he carve them, she found, but many he painted in colors that were true to life. She particularly adored a pair of Canada geese and cajoled him into letting her take them back to the cabin. He also showed her the toothpick models he built, explaining how he'd started making them for his own amusement. But one of his fur buyers had mentioned them to a couple from Boston, who then wanted a model made of their own stately home. The commission had launched Garrick into a leisurely business.

Leah thought his models were exquisite, particularly those dramatic designs he'd made for himself, on which he'd let his imagination go wild. "You could be an architect," she said, awed by the scope of that imagination and the detail he'd achieved with as unlikely materials as toothpicks.

He was pleased with her comment, but said nothing. He couldn't be an architect. He didn't have the training, for one thing, and for another, to get either that training or employment, he'd have to return to the city. The city—any city—was a threat to him. He'd be recognized. He'd be approached. He'd be tempted.

But he didn't tell Leah that. The words wouldn't seem to come. She loved him for who and what he was right now. He didn't want to disillusion her. He didn't want her to know what a mess he'd made of his earlier life. He feared that she'd think less of him, and the thought of losing her respect or, worse, her love, was more terrifying than anything.

But it bothered him that he didn't tell her the truth. Oh, he'd never lied. He'd simply ignored those seventeen years of his life as though they'd never been. That Leah hadn't asked puzzled him in some ways. They shared so many other thoughts and feelings. He suspected that she knew he harbored a dark secret and that she was afraid to ask for the same reason he was afraid to reveal it.

Perhaps because of that, neither spoke of the future. They took life one day at a time, treating their love as a precious gift that neither of them had expected to receive.

With her dictionary and thesauruses, an atlas and a world almanac on hand, Leah began to work. The peaceful setting was conducive to production, even in spite of the spate of questions Garrick bombarded her with at first.

"Where do you start?"

"On a puzzle? Wherever I want. If it's a theme puzzle—"

"Define theme puzzle."

"One in which the longer entries have to do with a specific topic."

"Like phrases depicting madness—having bats in one's belfry, etc.?"

She grinned, remembering that particular inspiration as he did. "Or names of baseball teams, or automobile models, or parts of the body."

"Oh?"

"Nothing naughty, of course. Once I did a puzzle using phrases like 'keep an eye on the ball,' 'put one's best foot forward,' 'give a hand to a friend'—that type of thing would be part of a theme puzzle."

"So you start with the theme?"

"Uh-huh, and I work from there."

He sat for a few minutes, silently watching her add words to her puzzle before he spoke again. "Do you follow a special formula regarding numbers of black and white spaces?"

She shook her head. "It can vary. The same holds true for checked and unchecked letters."

"Checked and unchecked?"

"Checked letters are ones that contribute to both an across and a down word, unchecked to only one or the other. In the earliest puzzles every letter was checked. If you got all the across clues, you had the puzzle completed."

"Too easy."

"Right. Nowadays, as a general rule of thumb, only fifty-five to seventy-five percent of the letters should be checked."

He digested that, then a bit later asked, "How about clues? Do you spend a lot of time finding them and revising them?"

"You bet. Again times have changed. It used to be that primary definitions were used. For example, the clue for 'nest' would be 'a bird's home.' In recent years, I've seen clues ranging from 'a place to feather' to 'grackle shack.' Actually," she added sheepishly, "my editor is a wonder when it comes to clever clues. I have no problem with her revisions."

"Do you ever have problems with deadlines?" Garrick asked, somewhat sheepish himself now. "I'm not letting you get much work done."

"I don't mind," she said, and meant every word.

In truth, as the days passed, Leah wondered if she was dreaming. Garrick was everything she'd ever wanted in a man. He was patient when she was working, attentive when she wasn't. He was interesting, always ready to discuss whatever topic crossed either of their minds. Even in cases of disagreement, the discussion was intelligent and ended with smiles. He was perceptive, suggesting they go out or make dinner or play checkers with the set he'd carved, just when she needed a break. He was positively gorgeous, tall and rangy, rugged with his full head of hair and his trimmed beard, compelling with his hazel-and-silver eyes. And he was sexy. So sexy. He turned her on with a look, a word, a move, and made love to her with passion, sometimes gently, sometimes fiercely, always with devotion.

The only thing to mar her happiness was the frown that crossed his face at odd moments, moments that became more frequent as the days passed.

Five days became a week, then ten days, twelve, two weeks. Garrick knew he had to tell her who he was. His fear remained, but the need for confession grew greater. He wanted her to know everything and to love him anyway. He wanted her to respect him for the way he'd rebuilt his life. He wanted—needed—to share past pain and present fear, wanted her understanding and support and strength.

Once, when the rain had stopped, he took her for a walk, intending to bare his soul while they were on the mountain. Then they caught sight of a doe and her fawn, and he didn't have the heart to spoil the scene.

Another time he led her off the mountain and they hitched a ride to town. He planned to confess all while they were splurging on lunch at the small restaurant there, but Leah was so enchanted by the charm of the place that he lost his nerve.

And then she insisted on calling Victoria. "I told her I'd give her a ring when I was settled. She may be worrying."

"Yeah, about whether you'll speak to her again after what she did."

"It didn't end up so terribly, did it?"

He grinned. "Nope. But maybe we ought to keep Victoria in suspense."

That was exactly what Leah did. From a pay phone inside the small general store, she dialed Victoria's number.

A very proper maid answered. "Lesser residence."

"This is Leah Gates. Is Mrs. Lesser in?"

"Please hold the phone."

Leah covered the mouthpiece and grinned at Garrick, who was practically on top of her, boxing her into the booth. "Can't you just picture Victoria? She's probably wearing an oversize work shirt and jeans, looking like a waif as she breezes round and about her elegant furnishings to reach the phone. I wonder what she's been doing. Playing the lute? Preparing sushi?" She removed her hand from the mouthpiece when Victoria's excited voice came on the other end.

"Where have you been?"

"Hi, Victoria."

"Leah Gates! I've been worried sick!"

Leah's eyes sparkled toward Garrick. "You shouldn't have worried. I told you I wouldn't have any problem. The cabin is wonderful. I can understand why Arthur loved it up here."

"Leah…"

"It's been a little rainy. That's why I didn't get around to calling sooner. My car is still mud-bound."

There was a pause. "Where are you calling from?"

"The general store."

Another pause. "How did you get there if your car is mud bound?"

"Hitched a ride."

"Leah!"

Garrick stole the receiver from Leah's hand. "Victoria?"

There was another brief silence on the other end of the line, then a cautious, "Garrick?"

"You play dirty pool."

"Ahh." A sigh. "Thank God. She's with you."

"As you intended."

"Do you hate me?"

"Not now."

"But you did at first. Please, Garrick, I only wanted the best for you both. You were alone. She was alone. I'm sure my letter explained—"

"I haven't read your letter." His eyes held Leah's, while the arm around her waist held her close.

"Why not?"

"I didn't want to."

"You were that angry? I didn't tell her anything about you, Garrick," she rounded defensively, then paused and lowered her voice. "Have you?"

"Some."

"But not…that?"

"No."

"She is staying with you?"

"I couldn't very well turn her out into the rain with nowhere to go," he said, a wink for Leah softening his gruff tone. Of course, Victoria didn't see the wink.

"Oh, Garrick, I'm sorry. I thought for sure you two would get along. You're so *right* for each other."

Garrick covered the mouthpiece and whispered to Leah, "She says we're so right for each other."

"Wise busybody," Leah whispered back, then grabbed the phone. "I won't be sending any rent money, Victoria Lesser."

"But you called. You can't be totally angry."

"I have more of a conscience than you do," Leah said, but she was smiling and Victoria knew it.

"Should I ready the green room for you?"

"Not just yet."

"You'll be staying there awhile?"

Leah didn't bother to cover the phone this time when she spoke to Garrick. Her free hand was drawing lazy circles on the firm muscles of his back. "She wants to know if I'll be staying here for a while."

He took the phone. "She'll be staying. I've discovered that I like having a live-in maid."

"I am *not* his maid," Leah shouted toward the mouthpiece, while Victoria added her own comment.

"Garrick, you are not to use Leah—"

"And a cook," Garrick injected. "She makes super egg foo yong."

"I do not make egg foo yong!" Leah protested, snatching the phone. "He's pulling your leg, Victoria."

Garrick grinned. "Another body phrase. Write it down, Leah."

"Leah, what is he talking about?"

"He's making fun of my cooking and my crossword puzzles. The man is impossible! See what you got me into?"

"Let me speak with Garrick, Leah."

Rather smugly, Leah handed over the phone.

"Garrick?"

"Yes, Victoria."

"Are we alone?"

"Yes."

"I don't want her hurt, Garrick."

"I know that."

"She's been through a lot. It's fine for you both to rib me—I deserve it. But I want you to treat her well, and that means using your judgment. If you'd read my letter, you'd know that she's totally trustworthy—"

"I didn't have to read your letter to learn that."

"If the two of you don't get along, I want her back here."

"We get along."

"Get along well?" Victoria asked hopefully.

"Yes."

"Well enough for a future?"

"I...maybe."

"Then you'll have to tell her, you know."

"I know."

"Will you?"

"Yes."

"If you wait too long, she'll be hurt."

"I know that, Victoria," he said soberly.

"I trust you to do the right thing."

"Yes," he said, then added, "Here's Leah. She wants to say goodbye. Say goodbye, Leah," he teased as he handed her the phone, but inside he was dying.

The right thing. The right thing. He had to tell her. But when?

7

As it happened, the truth spilled without any preplanning on Garrick's part, its disclosure as spontaneous as the rest of their relationship.

Leah had been with him for better than two weeks. On that particular morning they'd slogged through the mud to check on the progress of the beaver dam that had been growing steadily broader over a nearby stream. Later, returning to the cabin, they'd changed into clean, dry clothes and settled before the fire.

Garrick was reading one of the books Leah had brought with her from New York; they'd found they enjoyed discussing books they'd both read. Leah was close beside him on the sofa, her back braced against his arm, the soles of her feet flat against the armrest. She was listening to music, wearing the headset he'd salvaged from his nonfunctional CB and adapted for her cassette. On pure impulse, he set down his book and removed the earphones from her ears.

"Unplug it," he said over her forehead. "Let me hear."

She tipped back her head and met his gaze. "Ah, Garrick, you don't want to do that."

"Sure, I do."

"But you like the quiet."

"I want to hear your music. And besides, I don't like feeling cut off from you."

Turning, she came up on a knee and draped her arms around his neck. "You're not cut off. I keep the music low. I'd be able to hear you if you spoke."

"I want to hear your music," he insisted, wrapping his arms around her hips. "If you like it, I might like it, too. We have similar tastes."

"You hated the new Ludlum book that I loved."

"But we both agreed that Le Carré's was great."

"You hated that curried chicken we had the other night."

"Because I added too much curry. And don't say you didn't find it hot, because I saw you gulping down water."

"You hated the roadrunner I folded for you."

"I didn't hate it. I just didn't know what it was." He closed his fingers on a handful of her bottom and gritted his teeth in a pretense of anger. "Leah, I want to listen to music. Will you unplug the headset and let me hear?"

"You're sure?"

"I'm *sure.*"

Inwardly pleased, she removed the plug to the earphones. As the gentle sounds of guitar and vocalist filled the room, she sat back and watched Garrick's face.

He was smiling softly. "Cat Stevens. This is an old one."

"Seventy-four."

Sinking lower in the sofa, he stretched out his legs before him and listened quietly. He wore an increasingly pensive look, one that seemed to fade in and out, to travel great distances, return, then leave again. Leah knew the songs brought back memories, and when the tape was done, she would have been more than happy to put the machine away.

But he asked her to put on another tape. Again he recognized the song and its artists. "Simon and Garfunkel," he murmured shortly after the first bars had been sung.

"Do you like it?"

He listened a while longer before answering. "I like it. I've never paid much heed to the words before. I always associated songs like this with background music in restaurants."

"Where?" she asked, surprised at how easily the question came out.

"L.A.," he answered, surprised at the ease of his answer. It was time, he realized.

"Were you working there?"

"Yes."

"For long?"

"Seventeen years."

Leah said nothing more, but watched him steadily. When he swiveled his head to look at her, her heart began to thud. His eyes were dark, simultaneously sad, challenging and beseechful.

"I was an actor."

She was sure she'd heard him wrong. "Excuse me?"

"I was an actor."

She swallowed hard. "An actor."

"Yes." His eyes never left hers.

"Movies?" she asked in a small voice.

"Television."

"I...your name doesn't ring a bell."

"I used a stage name."

An actor? Garrick, the man she loved for his private life-style, an *actor?* Surely just occasionally. Perhaps as an extra. "Were you on often?"

"Every week for nine years. Less often before and after."

She swallowed again and twined her arms around her middle as though to catch her plummeting heart. "You had a major part."

He nodded.

"What's your name?"

"You know it. It's the one I was christened with."

"Your stage name."

"Greg Reynolds."

Leah paled. There wasn't a sound in the cabin; she felt more than heard her bubble of happiness pop. She'd never been a television fan, but she did have eyes. Even had she not had an excellent memory, she'd have been hard-pressed not to recall the name. It had often been splashed across the headlines of tabloids and magazines, glaring up from the stand at the grocery store checkout counter, impossible to miss even in passing.

"It can't be," she said, shaking her head.

"It is."

"I don't recognize you."

"You said you didn't watch television."

"I saw headlines. There must have been pictures."

"I look different now."

She tried to analyze his features, but they seemed to

waver. There was the Garrick she knew and…and then the other man. A stranger. Known to the rest of the world, not to her. She loved Garrick. Or was he… "You should have told me sooner."

"I couldn't."

"But…Greg Reynolds?" she cried in horror. "You're a star!"

"Was, Leah. Was a star."

She lowered her head and rubbed her forehead, trying to think, finding it difficult. "The show was…"

"*Pagen's Law.* Cops and robbers. Macho stuff—"

"That millions of people watched every week." She withered back into her corner of the sofa and murmured dumbly, "An actor. A successful actor."

Garrick was before her in an instant, prying her hands from her waist and enveloping them in his. "I *was* an actor, but that's all over. Now I'm Garrick Rodenhiser—trapper, Latin student, whittler, model maker—the man you love."

She raised stricken eyes to his. "I can't love an actor. I can't survive in the limelight."

He tightened his hold on her hands. "Neither can I, Leah. Greg Reynolds is dead. He doesn't exist anymore. That's why I'm here. Me. Garrick. This is my life—what you see, what you've seen since you've been here."

If anything, she sank deeper into herself. She said nothing, looked blankly to the floor.

"No!" he ordered, lifting her chin with one hand. "I won't let you retreat back into that shell of yours. Talk to me, Leah. Tell me what you're thinking and feeling."

"You were a phenomenal success," she breathed brokenly. "A superstar."

"*Was.* It's over!"

"It can't be!" she cried. "You can't stay away from it forever. They won't *let* you!"

"They don't want me, and even if they did, they don't have any say. It's my choice."

"But you'll *want* to go back—"

"No! It's over, Leah! I will not go back!"

The force of his words startled her, breaking into the momentum of her argument. Her eyes were large gray orbs of anguish behind the lenses of her glasses, but they held an inkling of uncertainty.

"I won't go back," Garrick said more quietly. His hand gentled on her chin, stroking it lightly. "I blew it, Leah. I can't go back."

The anguish wasn't hers alone. She saw in his eyes the pain she'd glimpsed before. It reached out to her, as it had always done, only now she had to ask, "What happened?"

For Garrick, this was the hard part. It was one thing telling her he'd been a success, another telling her how he'd taken success, twisted it, spoiled it, lost it. But he'd come this far. He owed it to Leah—and to himself—to tell it all.

Backing away from her, he stood and crossed stiffly to the window. The sun was shining, but the bleakness inside him blotted out any cheer that might have offered. Tucking his hands into the back of his waistband, he began to speak.

"I went out to the coast soon after I graduated from high school. It seemed the most obvious thing to do at the time. The one thing I wanted more than anything was to be noticed. I think you know why," he added more softly, but refrained from going into further self-analysis. "I had the goods. I was tall and attractive. I had the smarts that some others out there didn't have, and the determination. I just hung around for a while, getting a feel for the place, watching everything, learning who held the power and how to go about tapping it. Then I went to work. First, I talked a top agent into taking me on, then I willingly did whatever he asked me to do. Most of it was garbage—bit parts—but I did them well, and I made sure I was seen by the right people.

"By the time I'd been there three years, I was consistently landing reasonable secondary roles. But I wanted top billing. So I worked harder. I learned pretty quick that it wasn't only how you looked or acted that counted. Politics counted, too. Dirty politics. And I played the game better than the next guy. I kissed ass when I had to, slept around when I had to. I rationalized it all by saying that it was a means to an end, and I suppose it was.

"Five years after I arrived, I was picked to play Pagen." He lifted one shoulder in a negligent shrug. "Don't ask me why the show took off the way it did. Looking back on it, I can't see that it was spectacular. But it hit a vein with the public, and that meant money for the sponsors, the network, the producers, the directors and me. So we kept going and going, and in time I believed my own press. I convinced myself that the show was phenomenal and that it was phenomenal because of me."

He hung his head and took a shuddering breath. "That was my first mistake. No, I take that back. My first mistake was in ever going to Hollywood, because it wasn't my kind of place at all. Oh, I told myself it was, and that was my second mistake. My third mistake was in believing that I'd earned and deserved the success. After that the mistakes piled up, one after another, until I was so mired I didn't know which side was up."

He paused for a minute and risked a glance over his shoulder. Leah was in the corner of the sofa, her knees drawn up, her arms hugging her body. Her face seemed frozen in a stricken expression. He wanted to go down on his knees before her and beg forgiveness for who he'd been, but he knew that there was more he had to say first.

He turned to face her fully, but he didn't move from the window. "The show ran for nine years, and during that time I flared progressively out of control. I grew more and more arrogant, more difficult to deal with." His tone grew derisive. "I was the star, better than any of the others. I was the hottest thing to hit Hollywood in decades. What I touched turned to gold. My name alone could make the show—any show—a success.

"And there were other shows. After five years in the top ten with *Pagen,* I started making movies during the series' filming break. I fought it at first. I didn't know why at the time. Now I realize that something inside me was telling me that it was too much, that I needed a break from the rat race for a couple of months a year. That I needed to touch base for a short time with who I really was. But then I got greedy. I wanted to be more famous, and *more* famous. I wanted to become an indelible fixture in the entertainment world. I wanted to be a legend."

He sighed and bent his head, rubbing his neck with harsh fingers in an anger directed at himself. "I was running scared. That's really what it was all about. I was terrified that if I didn't grab it all while I had the chance, someone would come along and take it from me. But I wasn't all that good. Oh, I was Pagen, all right. I could play that part because it didn't take a hell of a lot of acting. Some of the other stuff—the movies—did, and I couldn't cut the mustard. None of them were box office hits, and that made me more nervous. Only instead of being sensible, taking stock and plotting a viable future for myself, I fought it. I berated the critics in public. I announced that the taste of the average moviegoer sucked. I got worse and worse on the set."

He looked at her then. "I was paranoid. I became convinced that everyone was waiting for me to fail, that they were stalking me, waiting to pounce and pick the flesh from my bones. I was miserable, so I began to drink. When that didn't help, I snorted coke, took whatever drugs I could get my hands on—anything that would blot out the unhappiness. All I succeeded in blotting out was reality, and in the entertainment world, reality means extraordinary highs and excruciating lows."

Taking a shuddering breath, he sighed. "*Pagen's Law* was canceled after a nine-year run, mostly because I'd become so erratic. The producers couldn't find directors willing to deal with me. They even had trouble gathering crews, because I was so impatient and demanding and critical that it just wasn't worth it. More often than not I'd show up on the set drunk or hung over, or I'd be so high on something else that I couldn't focus on the script. When that happened, I'd blame everyone in sight."

Very slowly he began to walk toward the sofa. His hands hung by his sides and his broad shoulders were slumped, but the desolation he felt was such that he simply needed to be near Leah. "It was downhill all the way from there. There were small parts after the series ended, but they came fewer and farther between. No one wanted to work with me, and I can't blame them. New shows took over where *Pagen* left off. New stars. The king was dead. Long live the king."

Very carefully he lowered himself to the sofa. His hands fell open, palms up in defeat, perhaps supplication, on his thighs. "In the end, I had no friends, no work. I was a pariah, and I had no one to blame but myself." He looked down at his hands and pushed his lips out. "I'd gotten so obsessed with the idea of being a star that I couldn't see any future if I didn't have that. So one day when I was totally stoned, I took my Ferrari and drove madly through the hills. I lost control on a turn and went over an embankment. The last thing I remember thinking was thank God it's over."

Leah's sharp intake of breath brought his gaze to hers. Her hands were pressed to her lips and her eyes were brimming with tears. He started to reach out, then drew back his hand. He needed to touch her, but he didn't know if he had the right. He was feeling as low, as worthless, as he'd felt when he'd awoken in that hospital after the accident.

"But it wasn't over," he said brokenly. "For some reason, I was spared. The doctors said that if I hadn't been so out of it, I'd have been more seriously hurt. I was loose as a goose when I was thrown from the car and ended up with only contusions and a couple of broken bones." His expression grew tight. "Someone had sent me a message, Leah. Someone was telling me that I hadn't spent thirty-six years of my life preparing for suicide, that there was more to me than that. I didn't hear it at first, because I was so wrapped up in self-pity that I couldn't think beyond it. But I had plenty of time. Weeks lying in that hospital bed. And eventually I came to accept what that someone was saying."

His voice lowered and his gaze softened on hers. "As soon as I could drive, I left L.A. I didn't know where I was going, only that I needed to get as far away from that world as possible. I kept driving, knowing that when I hit a comfortable place, I'd feel it. By the time I hit New Hampshire, I'd just about reached the end of the line.

"Then I saw this place. Victoria's husband had owned it—he used it for hunting parties—and Victoria kept it for a while after his death. Shortly before I came, she put it on the market through a local broker. From the first it appealed to me, so I bought it." He looked away. "It's odd how ignorant you can be of your own actions sometimes. Through all those years of success—of excess—the one thing I did right was to hire a financial adviser. He managed to invest the money I didn't squander, and he invested it wisely. I can live more than comfortably on the income from those investments without ever having to touch the capital."

He reached the end of his story, at least as far as the past was concerned. "I've made a life for myself here, Leah. I've been clean for four years. I don't touch alcohol or drugs, and I've sworn off indiscriminate sex." He looked at his hands, rubbed one set of long fingers with the other. "That other life wasn't me. If it had been, I wouldn't have botched it so badly. This is the kind of life I feel comfortable with. I can't—I won't—go back to the other."

Hesitantly his eyes met hers. "You're right. I should have told you all this sooner. But I couldn't. I was afraid. I still am."

Leah's cheeks were wet with tears, and her hands remained pressed to her lips. "So am I," she whispered against them.

Garrick did touch her then, almost timidly cupping her head. "You don't have to be afraid. Not of me. You know me better than any other person ever has."

"But that other man—"

"Doesn't exist. He never really did. He was a phony, an image, like everything else in Hollywood. An image with no foundation, so it was inevitable that it collapse. I don't want that kind of life anymore. You have to believe that, Leah. The only life I want is what I have here, what we've had here for the past two weeks. It's real. It's totally fulfilling—"

"But what about the need for public recognition? Doesn't that get in your blood?"

"It got in mine and nearly killed me. It was like a disease. And the cure was almost lethal, but it worked." He took a quick breath. "Don't let the mistakes I've made in the past turn you off. I've learned from them. Dear God, I've learned."

Leah wanted to believe everything he said. She wanted to believe it so badly that she began to shake, and her hands shot out to clutch his shoulders. "Greg Reynolds wouldn't be attracted to me—"

"Garrick Rodenhiser is."

"I'd be nothing in Greg Reynolds' world."

"You're everything in mine."

"I couldn't play games like that. I couldn't even play them for Richard."

"I don't want games. I want life. This life. And you."

Unable to remain apart from her a minute longer, he captured her mouth in a kiss that went beyond words in expressing his need. It was possessive and desperate and demanding, but Leah's was no less so.

"Don't ever be that other man," she begged against his mouth. "I think I'd want to die if you were."

"I won't, I won't," he murmured, then, while his hands held her head, took her mouth again and devoured it with a passion born of the love he felt. His lips opened wide, slanted and sucked, and he was breathing hard when he released her. "Let me love you," he whispered hoarsely, fingers working on the buttons of her shirt. "Let me give you everything I have…everything I've saved for you…everything that's come alive since you came into my life." Her shirt was open and his hands were greedily covering her breasts. "You're so good. All I've ever wanted."

Leah gave an urgent little cry and began to tug at his sweater. This was the Garrick she knew, the one who turned her on as no man ever had, the one who thought her beautiful and smart, the one who loved her. She felt as though she'd traveled from one end of the galaxy to the other since Garrick had begun his story. On a distant planet was the actor, but on progressively nearer ones was the man who'd suffered fear, then disillusionment, then pain. Even closer was the man who'd hit rock bottom and had begun to build himself up again. And here, with her, was the one who'd made it.

"I love you so," she whispered as his sweater went over his head. He brought her to his chest and held her there, rotating her breasts against the light matting of hair, then wrapping his arms around her and crushing her even closer.

He sighed into her hair, but that wasn't enough, so he kissed her again and again, then eased her back on the sofa and began to tug at her jeans. When her body was bare, he worshiped it with his mouth, dragging his tongue over her breasts and her navel, taking love bites from her thighs, burying his lips in the heart of her.

Leah's knuckles were white around the worn upholstery, her eyes closed tight against the sweet torment of his tongue against that ultrasensitive part of her. The world began to spin—this galaxy, another one, she didn't know—and her thighs tensed on either side of his head.

"Garrick!" she cried.

"Let it come, love," he whispered, his warm breath as erotic as his thrusting tongue.

Wave after wave of electrical sensation shook her, and she was still in the throes of glory when he opened the fly of his cords, stretched over her and thrust forward. She cried out again. Her knees came up higher. And it was like nothing she'd ever dreamed possible. Her climax went on and on—a second, then a third— while Garrick pumped deeply, reaching and achieving his own spectacular release.

He didn't leave her, but brought her up from the sofa until she was straddling his lap. And he began again, stroking more slowly this time, kissing her, dipping his head to lave her taut nipples with his tongue, using his hands to add extra sensation to the similarly taut nub between her legs, until it happened again and again and again.

Only when they were dripping with sweat and their bodies were totally drained did they surrender to the quiet after-storm where emotions raged. Leah cried. Damp-eyed himself, Garrick rocked her gently. Then, when she'd quieted, he pressed his lips to her cheek.

"I want to marry you, Leah, but I won't ask you now. Too much has happened today. It wouldn't be fair. But I'll be thinking it constantly, because it's the one thing that I want in life that I don't have right now."

Leah nodded against him, but she didn't breathe a word. She was sated, exhausted and happy. Yes, too much had happened today. But there was something else, something that went hand in hand with marriage that she hadn't told him. She had her secrets, too, and the burden of disclosure was now hers.

But the burdens had a way of falling from shoulders when one least expected them to. Such had been the case with Garrick's soul baring. Such was the case with Leah's.

A month had passed since she'd arrived at the cabin, one day blending into the next in a continual span of happiness. With the ebbing of mud season, Garrick's Cherokee was functional again. They drove into town for supplies, drove to the artists' colony, where Leah inquired about weaving lessons, drove to Victoria's cabin and freed the Golf, which Leah drove back to Garrick's and parked behind the cabin. They took long walks in the woods, often at daybreak when Garrick checked the few traps he'd set for coyotes, and picnicked in groves surrounded by the sweet smell of spring's rebirth.

Then, one morning, Leah awoke feeling distinctly muzzy. The muzziness passed, and she pushed it from mind, but the next morning it was back, this time accompanied by sharp pangs of nausea. When Garrick, who'd been fixing breakfast, saw her dash for the bathroom, he grew concerned. He followed her and found her hanging over the commode.

"What is it, sweetheart?" he asked, pressing a cool cloth to her beaded forehead.

"Garrick…oh…"

He supported her while she lost the contents of her stomach, then, very gently, closed the commode and eased her down. "What is it?" he repeated as he bathed her face. Her skin was ashen. His own hands shook.

"I didn't think it would happen…could happen…"

"What, love?"

She looked bewildered. "And I was never sick like this…"

"Leah?"

"Oh, God." She covered her face with her hands, then removed them to collapse against Garrick. "Hold me," she whispered tremulously. "Just hold me."

His arms were around her in an instant. "You're frightening me, Leah."

"I know…I'm sorry…. I think I'm going to have a baby."

For a minute he went very still. Then he began to tremble. Framing her face with his hands, he held her away from him and searched her eyes. "I thought," he began, "I guess I assumed that you…I shouldn't have… are you sure?"

"No."

"But you think so?"

"The nausea. I felt a little yesterday, too. And I haven't had a period." She was as bewildered as ever. "I didn't think…it was never like this."

"You weren't using birth control…an IUD?"

Her eyes were brimming with tears. "I've never had to worry about it. I always had trouble conceiving."

"Not now," Garrick said, pride and excitement surging within him. But something about what she'd said, and her expression, tempered his joy. "Have you conceived before?"

She nodded, then dissolved into tears.

Pressing her face into the warmth of his shoulder, he soothingly stroked her back. "What happened?" he whispered.

It was a while before she could answer, and when she did it was in a voice rife with pain. "Stillborn. I carried for nine months, but the babies were born dead."

"Babies?"

"Two. Two separate pregnancies. Both babies stillborn."

"Ahhhh, Leah," he moaned, holding her closer. "I'm sorry."

She was crying freely, but her words somehow found exit through her sobs. "I wanted…them so badly…and Richard did. He blamed me…even when the doctors said…I did nothing wrong."

"Of course you didn't do anything wrong. What did the doctors say caused it?"

"That was the…worst of it. They didn't know!"

"Shhhh. It's okay. Everything's going to be okay." As he held her and rocked her, a slow smile formed on his lips. A baby. Leah was going to have a baby. His baby. "Our baby," he whispered.

"I don't…know for sure."

"Well, we'll just have to find the nearest doctor and have him tell us for sure."

"It may be too early."

"He'll know."

"Oh, Garrick," she wailed, and started crying all over again. "I'm…so…frightened!"

He held her back and dipped his head so that they were on eye level with each other. His thumbs were braced high on her cheekbones, catching her tears. "There's nothing to be frightened of. I'm here. We'll be together through it all."

"You don't understand! I want your b-baby. I *want* your baby, and if something happens to it I don't know wh-what I'll do!"

"Nothing's going to happen. I won't let it."

"You can't *stop* it. No one could last time, or the time before that."

"Then this time will be different," he said with conviction. Scooping her into his arms, he carried her from the bathroom and set her gently back on the bed. "I want you to rest now. Later today we're going out to get a marriage license."

"No, Garrick."

"What do you mean, no?"

"I can't marry you yet."

"Because you're not sure if you're pregnant? I want to marry you anyway. You love me, don't you?"

"Yes."

"And I love you. So if you're pregnant, that'll be the frosting on the cake."

"But I don't want to get married yet."

"Why not?"

"Because I don't know if I can give birth to a living child. And if I can't, I'll always worry that you married me too soon and are stuck with me."

"That's the craziest thing I've ever heard. I *love* you, Leah. I told you two weeks ago that I wanted to marry you, and that was before there was any *mention* of a child."

"Don't you want children?"

"Yes, but I've never counted on them. Up until a month ago, I'd pretty much reconciled myself to the idea of living out my life alone. Then you came along and changed all that. Don't you see? Baby or no baby, having you with me is so much more than I've ever dreamed of—"

"Please," she begged. "Please, wait. For me." She pressed a fist to her heart. "*I* need to wait to get married. I need to know what's going to happen. If...if something goes wrong with the baby and you still want me, then I'll marry you. But I wouldn't be comfortable doing it now. If I am pregnant, the next eight-plus months are going to be difficult enough for me. If, on top of that, I have to worry about having my marriage destroyed..." Her voice dropped to an aching whisper. "I don't think I could take that again."

Garrick closed his eyes against the pain of sudden understanding. He dropped his head back, inhaled through flaring nostrils, then righted his head and very slowly opened his eyes. "That's what happened with Richard."

"Yes," she whispered.

"You mentioned other things—"

"There were. And maybe the marriage would have fallen apart anyway. But the baby—the babies—they were the final straw. Richard expected me to bear him fine children. They were part of the image—the wife, the home, the kids. The first time it happened we called it a fluke. But the second time, after all the waiting and praying and worrying—well, there was no hope left for us as a couple."

"Then he was a bastard," Garrick growled. "You could have adopted— No, forget I said that. If you'd done it, you'd probably still be married to him and then I wouldn't have you. I want you, Leah. If the babies come, I'll love it. If they don't and we decide we want children, we'll adopt. But we can't adopt a child unless we're married."

Leah closed her eyes. She was feeling exhausted, more so emotionally than physically. "I hadn't planned on getting pregnant."

"Some of the best things happen that way."

"I would rather have waited and had a chance to enjoy you more."

"You'll have that chance. Marry me, Leah."

Opening her eyes, Leah reached for his hand and slowly carried it to her lips. She kissed each one of his fingers in turn, then pressed them to her cheek. "I love you so much it hurts, Garrick, but I want to wait. Please. If you love me, bear with me. A piece of paper doesn't mean anything to me, as long as I know you're here. But that same piece of paper will put more pressure on me, and if I am pregnant, added pressure is the last thing I'll need."

Garrick didn't agree with her. He didn't see where their marrying would cause her stress, not given what he'd told her about his feelings. But he knew that she believed what she said, and since that was what counted, he had no choice but to accede.

"My offer still stands. If you're not pregnant, will you consider it?"

Feeling a wave of relief, she nodded.

"And if you are pregnant, if at any time over the next few months you change your mind, will you tell me?"

Again she nodded.

"If you are pregnant, I want to take a marriage license out before you're due to deliver. When that baby comes screaming and squalling into the world, it's going to have to wait for its first dinner until a judge pronounces us man and wife."

"In a hospital room?" Leah asked with a wobbly smile.

"Yes, ma'am."

She moved forward into his arms and coiled her own tightly around his neck. She loved the thought of that— a new husband, a healthy baby. She didn't dare put much stock in it, because she'd been let down on the baby part twice before, but it was a lovely thought. A very lovely thought.

8

Lovely thoughts had a way of falling by the wayside when other thoughts took precedence. That was what happened to Leah once the local doctor confirmed that she was pregnant. Her initial reaction was excitement, and it was shared with, even magnified by, Garrick's. Then the fear set in—and the concern, and the practical matter of how to deal with a new pregnancy after two had gone so awry.

"I'd like to speak to my doctor in New York," she said one night while she and Garrick were sitting thigh to thigh on the cabin steps. It had been a beautiful May day, marred only by Leah's preoccupation.

"No problem," Garrick said easily. "We can drive into town tomorrow to make the call. In fact, I've been thinking I'd like to have a phone installed here." It was something he'd never dreamed of doing before, but now that Leah was pregnant, concerns lurked behind his optimistic front. Having a phone would mean that help could be summoned in case of emergency.

Timidly she looked up at him. "I'd like to go back to New York." When he eyed her in alarm, she hurried on. "Just to see John Reiner."

"Weren't you comfortable with the doctor you saw here?"

"It's not that. It's just that John knows my medical history. If anyone can shed some light on what happened before and how to prevent it from happening again, it's him."

"Couldn't we just have Henderson call him?"

"I'd rather see John in person."

Garrick felt a compression around his heart, but it wasn't a totally new feeling. He'd been aware of it a lot lately, particularly when Leah's eyes clouded and she grew silent. "You're not thinking of having the baby in New York, are you?" he asked quietly.

"Oh, no," she answered quickly. "But for my peace of mind, I'd like to see John. Just for an initial checkup. He may be able to suggest something that I can do— diet, exercise, rest, vitamins—anything that will enhance the baby's chances."

Put that way, Garrick could hardly refuse. He wanted the baby as much as Leah did—more, perhaps, because he knew how much it meant to her. Still, he didn't like the idea of her leaving him, even for a few days. He didn't like the idea of her traveling to New York.

And he couldn't go with her.

"I don't want you driving down," he said. "You can take a plane from Concord. I'll have Victoria meet you at LaGuardia."

"You won't come?" she asked very softly. She had a feeling he wouldn't. Garrick didn't seem to dislike the city as much as he feared it. Even here she would have preferred seeing a doctor at a hospital, but that would have meant entering a city, and Garrick shunned even the New Hampshire variety. He'd insisted that she see a local man, though the closest one was a forty minute drive from the cabin. He hadn't even wanted to stop for dinner until they'd reached the perimeter of the small area in which he felt safe.

His eyes focused on the landscape, but his expression was one of torment. "No," he finally said. "I can't come."

Nodding, she looked down at her lap. "Can't" was something she'd have to work on. It was a condition in Garrick's mind and represented a fear that she could understand but not agree with. On the other hand, who was she to argue? Hadn't she been firm in putting off marriage? Hadn't Garrick disagreed, but understood and conceded?

"I'll have to call to make an appointment, but I'm sure he'll see me within the next week or so. I can make it a day trip."

That Garrick wouldn't concede to. "That's not wise, Leah. Lord only knows I don't want you gone overnight, but for you to rush would defeat the purpose. I don't want anything happening. If you have the pressure of flights and appointments, you'll be running all day. You'll end up tense and exhausted."

"Then I'll sleep when I get back," she protested. She didn't want to be away from Garrick any longer than was necessary. "The baby is fine at this stage. Even the fact that I've been sick is a good sign. Dr. Henderson said so. I didn't have any morning sickness with the other two."

But he was insistent. "Spend the night with Victoria. At least that way I won't worry quite as much."

* * *

So the following week she flew to New York, saw John Reiner, then spent the night at Victoria's. It should have been a happy reunion, and in many ways it was. Victoria was overjoyed that Leah and Garrick were in love, and she was beside herself when, promptly upon landing and in part to explain her doctor's appointment, Leah told her about the baby.

But some of the things that the doctor said put a damper on Leah's own excitement. She was feeling a distinct sense of dread when Garrick met her plane back in Concord the next afternoon.

"How do you feel?" he asked, leading her to the car. He'd called Victoria's on his newly installed phone the night before and knew that the doctor had pronounced Leah well, and definitely pregnant.

"Tired. You were right. It was a hassle. Hard to believe I used to live in that…and like it."

He had a firm arm around her shoulder. "Come on. Let's get you home."

She was quiet during most of the drive. With her head back and her eyes closed, she was trying to decide the best way to say what she had to. She didn't find an answer that night, because when they arrived back at the cabin, Garrick presented her with a small table loom and several instruction books on how to weave belts and other simple strips of cloth. She was so touched by his thoughtfulness that she didn't want to do anything to spoil the moment. Then, later, he made very careful, very sweet love to her, and she could think of nothing but him.

The next morning, though, she knew she had to talk.

It didn't matter that she was dying inside. What mattered was that their baby, hers and Garrick's, be born alive.

"Tell me, love," Garrick said softly.

Startled, she caught in her breath. She'd been lying on her back in bed, but at the sound of his voice her head flew around and her eyes met his.

He came up on an elbow. "You've been awake for an hour. I've been lying here watching you. Something's wrong."

She moistened her lips, then bent up an arm and shaped her fingers to his jaw. His beard was a brush-soft cushion; she took warmth from it and strength from the jaw beneath.

"John made a suggestion that I'm not sure you'll like."

"Oh-oh. He doesn't want us making love."

She gave a sad little grin and tugged at his beard. "Not that."

"Then what?"

She took a deep breath. "He thought that it would be better if I stay close to a hospital from the middle of my pregnancy on."

"'Stay close.' What does that mean?"

"It means live in the city. He gave me the name of a colleague of his, a man who left New York several years ago to head the obstetrics department at a hospital in Concord. John has total faith in him. He wants him to be in charge of the case."

"I see," Garrick said. He sank quietly back to the pillow and trained his gaze on the rafters. "How do you feel about it?"

Withdrawing her displaced hand, yet missing the contact, Leah said, "I want what's best for the baby."

"Do you want to move to the city?"

"Personally? No."

"Then don't."

"It's not as simple as that. My personal feelings come second to what's best for this baby's chances."

"What, exactly, did your doctor think that his man in Concord would be able to do?"

"Perform certain tests, more sophisticated ones than a local doctor is equipped to do. Closely monitor the condition of the baby. Detect any potential problem before it proves fatal."

Garrick had to admit, albeit begrudgingly, that that made sense. It was his baby, too. He didn't want anything to go wrong. "Didn't they do all that before?"

"Not as well as they can now. Nearly three years have passed. Medical science has advanced in that time."

"Well," he said, sighing, "we don't have to make a decision on it now, do we?"

"Not right away, I suppose. But John suggested that I see his man soon. They'll be in touch on the phone, and John will forward any records he thinks may be of help. Usually…" She hesitated, then pushed on. "Usually there'd be monthly appointments at this stage, but John wants me to be checked every two weeks."

Garrick shut his eyes tight. "That means tackling Concord every two weeks."

"Concord isn't so bad."

He said nothing.

"And besides, we're getting into good weather. It's

not such a long drive." But she knew that it wasn't the drive, or the weather, or any conflicting time demand that was the problem. "Will you drive me down twice a month?" she asked. She could easily drive herself, but she desperately wanted Garrick to be with her.

He didn't answer at first. In fact, he didn't answer at all. Instead he rolled toward her and took her into his arms. She felt the pulsing steel of his strength, smelled the musky, wood scent that was his and his alone, and when their lips met, she tasted his fear and worry…and love.

Garrick did drive her to Concord twice a month, but he was tense the whole way, and the instant each appointment was done, he quickly tucked her into the car and drove her home. Only on familiar turf was he fully at ease, but even that ease ebbed somewhat as late spring became early summer.

Outwardly life was wonderful. They shed sweaters and long pants for T-shirts and shorts, and more often than not, when he worked in the clearing around the cabin, Garrick was bare chested. Leah could have spent entire days just watching him. Sweat poured freely from his body. The muscles of his upper back and arms rippled with the thrust of a shovel or the swing of an ax. His skin turned a rugged bronze, while the sandy hue of his hair lightened. He was positively gorgeous and she told him so, which, to her surprise and delight, brought a deeper shade of red to his cheeks.

He put in his garden and spent long hours cultivating it. During those times Leah sat near him, either watching, weaving, basking in the sun or working on puzzles. She was regularly shipping parcels off to New York, and the fact that there was now a phone at the cabin facilitated communications with her editor. The queasiness and fatigue that had initially slowed her down had passed by the end of June; come July, she was feeling fine and beginning to show.

They were as deeply in love as ever. Leah made a point of protesting when Garrick doted on her, but she drank in his attention and affection. In turn, she did whatever she could to make his days special, but she had a selfish motive, as well. The busier she was, the more dedicated to his happiness, the less she thought about the child growing inside her.

She didn't want to think about it. She was frightened to pin hopes and dreams on something that might never be. In mid-July she underwent amniocentesis, and though she was relieved to learn that, at that point at least, the baby was healthy, she didn't want to know its sex.

Neither did Garrick. There were times when he was working the soil or whittling or listening to Leah's music when his mind would wander. At those odd moments he had mixed feelings about the baby. Oh, he wanted it; but he resented it, too, for in his gut he knew Leah was going to leave. She didn't say so. They deliberately avoided discussion of what was to come in August, when she reached the midway point of her pregnancy. But he knew what she was thinking when her eyes lowered and her brow furrowed, and he dreaded the day when she'd finally broach the subject.

More than anything he would have liked to stop time. He'd have Leah. He'd have the baby thriving inside her. He'd have the bright summer sunshine, the good, rich earth, the endless bounty of the mountain. He didn't want things to change; he liked them as they were. He felt safe and secure, productive and well loved.

But he couldn't stop time. The heat of each day turned to the chill of evening. The sun set; darkness fell. The baby inside Leah grew until her abdomen was as round as the cabbage he'd planted in the garden. And when Leah approached him in the middle of August, he knew that his time of total satisfaction was over.

"We have to talk," she said, sitting down beside him on the porch swing he'd hung. She'd gone inside for a sweater to ward off the cool night air; it was draped over the T-shirt—Garrick's T-shirt—that covered the gentle bubble of her stomach.

"I know."

"Dr. Walsh wants me closer to the hospital."

He nodded.

"Will you come?"

Looking off toward the woods, Garrick took a deep breath. When he spoke, his voice was gritty. "I can't."

"You can if you want."

"I can't."

"Why not?"

"Because this is my home. I can't live in the city again."

"You can if you want."

"No."

"I'm not asking you to move there for good. It would be for four months at most. Dr. Walsh is planning to take the baby by section in the middle of December."

Garrick swallowed. "I'll be with you then."

"But I want you with me now."

He looked at her sharply. "I can't, Leah. I just can't."

Leah was trying to be understanding, but she had little to work with. "Please. Tell me why."

He bolted up from the swing, and in a single stride was leaning against the porch railing with his back to her. "There's too much to do here. Fall is my busy time. Trapping season opens at the end of October. There's a whole lot to do before then."

"You could live with me part-time in Concord. It'd be better than nothing."

"I don't see why you have to live in Concord. I drive. The Cherokee is dependable. If there's a problem, I could have you at the hospital in no time."

"Garrick, it takes *two hours* to get there. Both times before, things went wrong after I'd gone into labor. Those two hours could be critical."

"We have a phone. We could call an ambulance… or…or call for a police escort if there's a need."

"Ambulance attendants don't have the know-how to handle problem deliveries. Neither do police."

"Okay," he said, turning to face her. "Then we can go to Concord in November. Why September?"

"Dr. Walsh wanted August, but I put him off."

"Put him off for another few months."

Tugging the sweater closer around her, Leah studied the planked floor of the porch. "Do you want this baby, Garrick?"

"That's a foolish question. You know I do."

"Do you love me?"

"Of course!"

She looked up. "Then why can't you do this for me—for the baby—for all three of us?"

With a low growl of frustration, he turned away again. "You don't understand."

"I think I do," she cried, pushing off from the swing and coming up to where he stood. "I think you're frightened—of people, of the city, of being recognized. But that's ridiculous, Garrick! You've made a good life for yourself. You have *nothing* to be ashamed of."

"Wrong. I spent seventeen years of my life behaving like a jackass."

"But you paid the price, and you've rebuilt your life. So what if someone recognizes you? Are you ashamed of who you are now?"

The pale light of the moon glittered off the flaring silver flecks in his eyes. "No!"

"Why can't you go out there and hold your head high?"

"It's got nothing to do with pride. What I have now is much finer than anything I had then. *You're* much finer than any woman I knew then."

"What is it, then? What is it that makes you nervous each and every time we approach civilization? I've seen it, Garrick. Your shoulders get tense. You keep your head down. You avoid making eye contact with strangers. You refuse to go into restaurants. You want to get out of wherever we are as quickly as possible."

"It bothers you not going out on the town?"

"Of course not! What bothers me is that you're uncomfortable. I love you. I'm proud of you. It hurts me to see you slinking around corners as though there's—" she faltered, searching for an analogy "—as though there's a trap set around the next one."

"I know all about traps. Sometimes you don't see them until you're good and caught."

"Then there's the case of the coyote, who won't be caught in the same place twice."

"The coyote's an animal. I'm human."

"That's right. You're smart and fine and strong—"

"Strong? Not quite." He turned to face her. The faint glow spilling from inside the cabin side-lit his features, adding to the harshness of his expression. "What I had for seventeen years was a disease, Leah. It was an addiction. And the one thing a former addict doesn't do is let the forbidden be waved before his nose. I won't go into restaurants with bars because I'd have to walk by all those bottles to get to a seat. I won't look people in the eye because if they were to recognize me I'd see their star lust. I don't watch television. I don't go to movies. And the last thing I wanted when you came here was heavy sex." He snorted. "Guess I blew it on that one."

"You don't trust yourself," she said, at last comprehending the extent of his fear.

"Damn right, I don't. When you first showed up, I thought you were a reporter. I wanted to get rid of you as soon as possible, and you want to know why? If a reporter—especially a pretty one—were to interview me, I'd feel pretty important. And then I'd get to thinking that I'd done my penance for screwing up once, and maybe I should try for the big time again."

"But you don't *want* that anymore."

"When I'm here I don't. When I'm thinking rationally, I don't. But I spent a good many years thinking irrationally. Who's to say that I wouldn't start doing it again?"

"You wouldn't. Not after all you've been through."

"That's what I tell myself," he said in a weary tone, "but it's not a hundred percent convincing." He thrust a handful of fingers through his hair, which fell back to his forehead anyway. "I don't know how I'd react face to face with temptation."

She slipped her hand under the sleeve of his T-shirt to his shoulder. "Don't you think it's time you tried? You can't go through the rest of your life living under a shadow." She gave him a little shake. "You've been happy here. You feel good about your life. Wouldn't it be nice to prove to yourself, once and for all, that you have the strength that *I* know you have?"

"You love me. You see me through rose-coloured glasses."

Leah's hand fell away as she tamped down a spurt of anger. "My glasses are untinted, thank you, and even if they weren't, that's a lousy thing to say. Yes, I love you. But I've been through love once before, and I'm a realist. I entered this relationship with my eyes wide open—"

"You're nearsighted."

"Not where feelings and emotions are concerned. Oh, I can see your faults. We all have them, Garrick. That's what being human is about. But you took on your weaknesses once before and came out a winner. Why can't you take on this last one?"

"Because I might fail, damn it! I might face temptation and succumb, and where would that leave me, or you, or the baby?"

"It won't happen," she declared quietly.

"Is that an ironclad guarantee?"

"Life doesn't come with guarantees."

"Right."

"But you have so much more going for you now than you had before," she argued. "You have the life you've made, and it's one you love. And you have me. I wouldn't sit idly back and watch you fall into a pattern of self-destruction. I don't want that other life any more than you do. And I don't want you hurt. I *love* you, Garrick. Doesn't that mean anything?"

He bowed his head and, in the shadows, groped blindly for her hand. "It means more than you could ever imagine," he said hoarsely, weaving his fingers through hers, holding them tightly.

"Come with me," she pleaded. "I know it's asking a lot, because it cuts into the trapping season, but you don't need the money. You said so yourself. And these are extenuating circumstances. It won't happen every year. It may never happen again."

"God, Leah…"

"I need you."

"Maybe you need something I don't have to give."

"But you're a survivor. Look at what you've been through. It isn't every man who can land in a canyon, half-broken in body and more than that in spirit, and rise again to be the kind of person who can—" again she floundered for words "—can take in a bedraggled mess of mud from your doorstep half suspecting that she was planning to stab you in the back with a poison pen story."

He made a noise that, in other circumstances and with a stretch of the imagination, might have been a laugh. "You were a little pathetic."

"The point is," she went on, "that your heart's in the

right place. You want the best—for you, for me, for the baby. You can do anything you set your mind to. You can *give* anything you want."

Closing his eyes, Garrick put a hand to the tense muscles at the back of his neck. He dropped his head to the side, then slowly eased it back and around. "Ahhh, Leah. You make it sound so simple. Perhaps I could do it if I had you by my side every minute, whispering in my ear like a Jiminy Cricket. But I can't do that. I won't. I need to stand on my own two feet. Here I can do it."

"You asked me to marry you. Are you saying that we'd never take a vacation, never go somewhere different?"

"If it bores you to be here—"

"It doesn't, and you know it! But everyone needs a change of scenery sometimes. Suppose, just suppose this baby lives—"

"It *will* live," he barked.

"See, you can be optimistic, because you haven't been through the hell I have once, let alone twice. But I'm willing to try again—"

"It happened. We didn't plan it."

"I could have had an abortion."

"You're not that kind of person."

"Just as you're not the kind of person who gave up on life when you came to in that hospital. You could have, y'know. You could have gone right back to drinking and taking whatever else you were taking, but you didn't. You were willing to make a stab at a new life. Some people wouldn't have the courage to do that, but you did. All I'm asking now is that you take it one step further." She gave a frustrated shake of her head. "But that wasn't what I wanted to say. I wanted to say that if the baby lives, and grows and gets more active and demanding, there may be times when I'll want to go off with my husband somewhere, alone, just the two of us. Maybe to somewhere warm in winter, or somewhere cool in summer. Or maybe I'll want to go somewhere adventurous—like Madrid or Peking or Cairo. It would have nothing to do with being bored here, or not loving our child, but simply a desire to learn about other things and places. Would you refuse?"

He was silent for a minute. "I haven't thought that far."

"Maybe you should."

He eyed her levelly. "Before I mention marriage again?"

"That's right."

"Are you issuing an ultimatum, Leah?"

She turned her head aside in disgust. "An ultimatum? Me? I've used the word dozens of times in puzzles, but I wouldn't know how to apply it in real life if I had to." Removing her glasses, she rubbed the bridge of her nose. "No ultimatum," she murmured. "Just something to think about, I guess."

When she didn't raise her head, Garrick did it for her. The tears that had gathered in her eyes wrenched his insides, but he said what he had to say. "I love you, Leah. That won't change, whether you're here or in Concord. But I can't go with you. Not now. Not yet. There are still too many things I have to work out in my mind. I want to marry you, and that won't change, either, but maybe it would be good if we were separated for a time. If you're in Concord, under Walsh's eye, I'll know you're well cared for. While you're there, you'll be able to think about whether I *am* the kind of man you want. Except for two days, we've been together constantly for nearly five months. If it were fifty months or years, I'd still feel the same about you. But you have to accept me for what I am. Baby or no baby, you have a right to happiness. If my shortcomings are going to prevent that down the road, then…maybe you should do some rethinking."

Leah didn't know what to say, which was just as well, because her throat was so clogged she wouldn't have been able to utter a word. There were things she wanted to say, but she'd already said them, and they hadn't done much toward changing Garrick's mind. She'd never been one to nag or harp, and she refused to resort to that now. So she simply closed her eyes and let herself be enfolded in his arms, where she etched everything she loved about him into memory for the lonely period ahead.

She left the next day while Garrick was out on the mountain. It didn't take her long to pack, since she had a limited supply of maternity clothes. The things she wanted most were her resource books, her music and her loom, and these she carried to the car in separate trips. She worked as quickly as she could, pausing at the end to leave a short note.

"Dear Garrick," she wrote, "We all have our moments of cowardice, and I guess this is mine. I'm on my way to Concord. I'll call you tonight to let you know where I'll be staying. Please don't be angry. It's not that I'm choosing the baby over you, but that I want you both. You've said that you'll love me no matter where I am, and I'm counting on that, because I feel the same. But I want a chance to love a child of ours, and I want you to have that chance, too. That's why I have to go." She signed it simply, "Leah."

Though she didn't have an appointment set up for that particular day, Gregory Walsh saw her shortly after she arrived.

"Aren't you feeling well?" he asked as soon as she was seated.

She forced a small smile. "I'm feeling fine, but I…need a little help. I've just driven in. All my things are still in the car. I'm…afraid I haven't planned for this very well. It seems—" she grimaced "—that I don't have a place to stay. You're familiar with the area around the hospital. I was hoping you could suggest an apartment or a duplex, something furnished that I could rent."

Walsh was quiet for several minutes, his kindly eyes gentle, putting her at ease as they had from the start. "You're alone," he said at last, softly and without condemnation.

Her gaze fell to her twisting thumbs. "Yes."

"Where's Garrick?"

"Back at the cabin."

"Is there a problem?"

"Not really. He just didn't feel that he could…be here for such a long stretch."

"How do you feel about that?"

"Okay."

"Really?"

"I guess."

Again the doctor was silent, this time steepling his fingers beneath his chin and pursing his lips. His eyes remained on her bowed head. When he spoke at last, his voice was exquisitely gentle. "People often assume that my job is purely physical, examining one pregnant lady after another, prescribing vitamins, delivering babies. There's much more to it than that, Leah. Pregnancy is a time of change, and it brings with it a wide range of emotional issues. It's my job—and wish—to deal with some of those issues. From a medical standpoint, a more relaxed mother-to-be is a healthier one, and her baby is healthier." He lowered his hands. "Given your medical history, you have had more than your share of worries. Having you close by the hospital gives me a medical edge, but I was also hoping that it would serve to ease your fears."

She raised her head. "It will. That's why I'm here."

"But you've always been with Garrick before. It'd take a blind man not to see how close you two are. It'd take an insensitive one not to guess that it bothers you he's not with you now. I'd like to think I'm neither blind nor insensitive. I'd also like to think that you feel comfortable enough with me to tell me, honestly, what you're feeling."

"I do," she said softly. She didn't know how one could *not* feel comfortable with a man like Gregory Walsh. In his early fifties, he was pleasant to look at and talk with. He seemed to have a sensor fine-tuned to his patients' needs; he knew when to speak and when to listen. She'd never once sensed any condescension on his part, quite a feat given his position.

"Then tell me what you really feel about Garrick's staying behind at the cabin."

She thought for a minute, and when she spoke, her voice was unsteady. "I feel…lots of things."

"Tell me one."

"Sadness. I miss him. It's only been a few hours, but I miss him. Not only that, but I picture him alone back at the cabin and I hurt for him. I know it's stupid. It was his choice to stay there, and besides, he's a big boy. He lived there alone for a long time before I arrived. He's more than capable of taking care of himself. Still, I…it bothers me."

"Because you love him."

"Yes."

He nodded in encouragement. "What else are you feeling?"

She grew pensive and frowned. "Dismay. I've lived alone, too. I've taken care of myself. Yet here I am, all but crying on your doorstep, not knowing where I'm going to spend the night. I feel…handicapped."

"You're pregnant. That has to make any woman feel a little more vulnerable than usual."

"That's it. Vulnerable. I do feel that."

"What else?"

She lifted one shoulder and tipped her head to the side, her eyes dropping back to her hands. "Anger. Resentment. Garrick has his reasons for doing what he is, and I'm trying to understand them, but right about now it's hard."

"Because you're feeling alone?"

"Yes."

"And a little betrayed?"

"Maybe. But I don't have a right to feel that. Garrick never said he'd come. In all the time I've known him, he's never promised anything he hasn't delivered."

"You can still feel betrayed, Leah. It's normal."

"He was the one who wanted to get married."

"Has he changed his mind?"

"No. But even if we were married, I doubt he'd be here. He has a certain…hang-up. I can't explain it."

"You can, but you won't, because that would be betraying him," Walsh suggested with an insight that drew her grateful gaze to his. "I respect you for that, Leah. And anyway, I don't pretend to be a psychiatrist. All I want to do is help you out where I can. Will you be in touch with Garrick while you're here?"

"I told him I'd call tonight. He'll worry otherwise."

"Will he be down to visit?"

"I don't know. He said he'd be here when the baby's due."

"Well, then, that's something to look forward to. The anger, the resentment, the sense of betrayal—those are things you and Garrick will have to work out. All I can say is that you shouldn't deny them or feel guilty for feeling them." He held up a hand. "I'm not criticizing Garrick, mind you. I haven't heard his side of the story, and I wouldn't deign to imagine what's going on in his mind."

"He probably feels betrayed himself, because I chose to come here instead of staying with him. I do feel guilty about that, but I had no choice!"

"You did what you felt you had to do. That's your justification, Leah. It doesn't mean that you have to like the situation. But if you were to drive back to him right now you'd probably show up on my doorstep again tomorrow. In your heart, you feel that what you're doing is best for the baby. Am I right?"

She answered in a whisper. "Yes."

"So. I want you to keep telling yourself that." He grinned unexpectedly. "As for feeling alone and having nowhere to stay, I think I have a perfect solution. My place."

"Dr. Walsh!"

He laughed. "I love it when gorgeous young women take me the wrong way. Let me explain. My wife and I moved up here when the last of our boys—we have four—graduated from college. They were all out doing their own thing, and we felt it was time we did ours. We liked New York, but progressively it was getting more difficult for Susan—that's my wife—to handle. She has crippling arthritis and is confined to a wheelchair."

Leah gasped. "I'm sorry."

"So am I. But, God bless her, she's a good sport about it. She never complained in New York, but I knew that she'd love to be in a place where she could go in and out more freely. When the offer came from this hospital, I grabbed it. We bought a house about ten minutes from here." He chuckled. "In New York that would still be city. Here it's a quiet, tree-shaded acre. One of the things we loved about the house was that there was an apartment in what used to be a garage. Separate from the house. Set kind of back in the trees. We thought it would be ideal for when the boys came to visit. And they do come, but never for more than a night here or there, and then they usually sleep on the living room couch." He sat forward. "So, the apartment's yours if you want it. You'd be close to the hospital but away from the traffic. And Susan would love the company."

Leah was dumbfounded. "I couldn't impose—"

"You wouldn't be imposing. You'd be in your own self-contained unit, and I'd know you were comfortable."

"Is it wise for a doctor to be doing this for a patient?"

"Wise? Let me tell you, Leah. There's another reason I left New York, and that was because I was tired of the internal politics at a large city hospital. Here I do what I want. I decide what's wise. And yes, I think my offer is wise, just as I think you'd be wise to take me up on it."

"I'd want to pay rent," she said, then winced. "The last time I said that, I got to where I was going and found it demolished."

"This place isn't demolished, and you can pay rent if it will make you feel better."

"It will," she said, smiling. "Thank you, Dr. Walsh."

"Thank *you*. You've just made my day." At her questioning look, he explained. "When I can make a patient smile, particularly one who walked in here looking as sober as you did, I know I've done something right."

"You have." Her smile grew even wider. "Oh, you have."

9

The apartment was as perfect as Gregory Walsh had said it would be. With walls dividing the space into living room, bedroom and kitchenette, it seemed smaller than the cabin, but it was cozy. The furnishings were of rattan, and where appropriate, there were cushions in pale blue and white, with draperies to match, giving a cheerful, yet soothing effect. Leah had free access to the yard, which was lush in the wild sort of way that reminded her of the woods by the cabin and made her feel more at home.

Susan Walsh was an inspiration. "Good sport" was a mild expression to describe her attitude toward life; her disposition was so sunny that Leah couldn't help but smile whenever they were together, and that was often.

But there were lonely times, times when Leah lay in bed at night feeling empty despite the growing life in her belly. Or times when she sat in the backyard, trying to work and being unable to concentrate because her mind was on Garrick. He called every few days, but the conversation was stilted, and more often than not she'd hang up the phone feeling worse than ever.

The desolation she felt stunned her. She'd never

minded when, during each of her previous pregnancies, Richard had gone off on business trips. She tried to tell herself that her separation from Garrick was a sort of business trip, but it didn't help. Garrick wasn't Richard. Garrick had found a place in her heart and life that Richard had never glimpsed. She missed Garrick with a passion that six months before she wouldn't have believed possible.

Physically, she did well. She saw Gregory at the hospital for biweekly appointments. His examinations grew more thorough and were often accompanied by one test or another. She didn't mind them, for the results were reassuring, as was the fact that the hospital was close should she feel any pang or pressure that hinted at something amiss. She didn't feel anything like that, only the sporadic movements of the baby, movements that became stronger and more frequent as one week merged into the next.

She wanted Garrick to feel those sweet little kicks and nudges. She wanted him to hear the baby's heartbeat, as she had. But she knew she couldn't have it all. In her way, she had made a choice. The problem was learning to live with it.

Then shortly before dawn one morning, after she'd been in Concord for nearly a month, she awoke to an eerie sensation. Without opening her eyes, she pressed a hand to her stomach. Her pulse had automatically begun to race, but she couldn't feel anything wrong. No aches or pains. No premature contractions. She was barely breathing, waiting to identify what it was that had awoken her, when light fingers touched her face.

Eyes flying wide, she bolted back and screamed.

"Shhhhh." Gentle hands clasped her shoulders. "It's just me."

All Leah could make out was a blurred form in the pale predawn light. "Garrick?" she whispered as she clutched frantically at the wrists by her shoulders. He felt strong like Garrick. He smelled good like Garrick.

"I'm sorry I frightened you," said the gravelly voice that was very definitely Garrick's.

She threw her arms around his neck and held him for a minute, then, unable to believe he was really squatting by her bedside, pushed back and peered at him. She needed neither her glasses nor a light to distinguish each of the features she'd missed so in the past weeks.

"Frightened? You *terrified* me," she exclaimed in a hoarse whisper. "What are…why are you…at this hour?"

He shrugged and gave a sheepish smile. "It took me longer than I thought to get everything packed."

"Packed?" Her fingers clenched the muscles at the back of his neck. "Are you—"

"Moving in with you? Yes. I figured you owed me."

Softly crying his name, she launched herself at him again. This time she hung on so relentlessly that he had to climb into bed with her to keep from being choked to death.

He didn't mind. Any of it. "I've been in agony, Leah," he confessed in a ragged whisper. "You've ruined the cabin for me. I'm miserable there without you. And those phone calls suck."

She couldn't restrain an emotional laugh. "Ditto for me. To all of it."

"You weren't at the cabin. You don't know how empty it was."

"I know how empty *I've* been." Her mouth was against his throat. "But what about…you were so adamant about not coming…"

"You said the word in the note you left. Cowardice. It nagged at me and nagged at me until I couldn't take it anymore. I don't know what's going to happen to me here, but I have to take the chance. I don't have any other choice. Being with you means too much."

With a soft moan of heavenly thanks, she began to kiss him—his neck, his beard, his cheekbones, eyes and nose. By the time she'd reached his mouth, she was bunching up his jersey, dragging it from the waistband of his jeans. Her progress was impeded briefly by his hands, which were all over her body, then homing in on those places that had altered most during their separation.

"I want you badly," he groaned. "Can we?"

"Yes, but—"

"Let me make love to you."

"You already have by coming here," she whispered, her breath hot against his skin. She was kissing his chest, moving from one muscled swell to the next, one tight nipple to the other. "Now it's my turn."

Garrick couldn't stop touching her, but he closed his eyes and lay back. He raised his hips when she unzipped his jeans and kicked his legs free after she'd peeled them down.

Leah loved him as she'd never done before. Her appetite was voracious, and the small sounds of pleasure that came from his throat made her all the more bold. His hands were restless in her hair, on her shoulders and back, and while she touched him everywhere, kissed him everywhere, he squeezed his eyes shut against the agony of ecstasy. When she took him into her mouth, he bucked, but her hands were firm on his hips, holding him steady for the milking of lips and tongue. The release he found that way was so intense, so shattering for them both, that the first rays of the sun were poking through the drapes before either of them could speak.

"You make me feel so loved," he whispered against her forehead.

"You are," she returned as softly. "I hadn't realized how much of my time at the cabin was spent showing you that—until I got here and didn't know what to do with myself."

He moved over her then, fingers splayed on either side of her head, eyes wide and brilliant. "You… have… no idea how much I love you."

"I think I do," she said with a soft smile. "You're here, aren't you?"

"Yes. And I intend to make it. For you."

"No, for *you*."

"And for you."

"Okay, for me."

"And for baby," he said, lowering a hand to properly greet his child.

Leah let Garrick find his own pace in Concord. She would have been happy if he just sat with her in the yard or the apartment and accompanied her to the hospital for her appointments. But he did more than that. Within days of his arrival, he signed up to take several courses at the local university. She knew that the first few trips he made there were taxing for him, because he returned to her pale and tired. But he stuck with it, and in time he felt less threatened.

Likewise, he insisted on taking her for walks each day. Gregory had recommended the exercise, and though they began with simple neighborhood trips, Leah's eagerness and Garrick's growing confidence soon had them covering greater distances. Often Garrick wheeled Susan in her chair while Leah held lightly to his elbow; other times Leah and Garrick went alone.

"How do you feel?" Leah asked on one of those private outings.

"Not bad."

"Nervous?"

"Not really. No one seems to recognize me. No one's looking twice." He snorted. "If I had any brains, I suppose I'd be offended."

"It's because you do have brains that you're not. How about at school? Have there been any double takes there?"

"No." He didn't tell her about the anxiety he'd felt when, during one of those very tense first days of class, he'd stood for five minutes outside a local tavern, aching for a drink, just one to calm him down. Nor did he tell her of the flyers he'd seen posted around the university, advertising dramatic productions in the works; he'd stared at those, too, for a very long time.

But he was with her, and he was doing all right, and *she* was doing all right, which was what really mattered.

Mid-October brought the turning of the leaves. Garrick would have liked to show Leah the brilliance of the autumnal spectacle from the cabin, but he didn't dare make even a day trip back to the mountain. The baby was growing bigger and Leah's body more unwieldy; in terms of both comfort and safety, he knew that she was better off staying in Concord.

November brought a marked downshift in the temperature, as well as Garrick's insistence that he and Leah file for a marriage license. It also brought orders from Gregory soon after, that Leah was to stay in bed. She wasn't thrilled with the prospect, for it meant an end to her outings with Garrick. And that she'd have more time on her hands to worry about the baby.

She'd had every test imaginable. Gregory had made detailed comparisons between the results of those tests and the information gleaned from less frequent and less detailed tests done during her last pregnancy in New York. All signs were good, he declared. The baby appeared to be larger, the heartbeat stronger than ever.

"I think you've planted a monster in me," she complained to Garrick one afternoon when she felt particularly uncomfortable.

"Like father, like son," he teased.

"Ah, but we don't know that. What if we get an amazon of a daughter?"

"She can be a Cyclops, for all I care, as long as she's healthy."

Which was the password. Healthy. Boy or girl, they didn't care, as long as the child was born alive.

Increasingly, though she warned herself not to, Leah did think about the child—what sex it was, what they would name it, whether it would have Garrick's eyes or her hair, whether it would like to read. And the more she daydreamed, the more nervous she became, for the critical time was fast approaching.

Garrick, too, was growing nervous, and only part of it had to do with the coming delivery. When he was on campus, he found himself drawn more and more often to the building that housed the small theater. Any number of times he simply stood outside and stared at it. Then one day, with his hands balled into fists in the pocket of his high-collared jacket, he ventured inside.

The theater was dim, with rows and rows of vacant seats, one of which he slipped into while he trained his eyes on the lit stage. Though he'd never acted in a classic himself, he knew Chekov when he saw it. The set was distinct, as were the lines. Slouching lower, he propped his chin on a fist and watched the fledgling actors and actresses do their thing.

They were impressive, he decided after a time. Not quite there yet, but on their way. They were interrupted from time to time by the director, a woman whose voice he could hear, though he couldn't see her. The students were attentive, listening quietly to her criticism, then attempting to follow her suggestions. Sometimes they succeeded; sometimes they didn't. But they tried.

Garrick wondered what would have happened if *he'd* tried the way they did. He wondered whether, if he'd listened to directors, perhaps taken formal acting instruction, he would have been able to evolve into a truly good actor. He'd never really given it a shot. *Pagen* had come along and made him a star, so he hadn't had to.

Watching the young performers, he wondered if any of them dreamed of being stars. More aptly, he wondered if any of them *didn't*. He focused on one young man whose voice wasn't quite forceful enough but whose interpretation was a bit more compelling than that of the others. What would he do after college? Go to New York? Work off-Broadway for a while? Make it to Broadway itself? Or think beyond all that and high-tail it to the coast, as he'd done?

His eyes skimmed the stage again, this time alighting on a girl, blond haired and petite of build. As she moved the faint bobbing of her breasts was visible beneath an oversize sweatshirt that tucked snugly under her bottom. He wondered whether she was having an affair with one of the boys—perhaps the good-looking one standing off by the wings? If so, it probably wouldn't last. If her career surpassed his, she'd leave him behind and move on. To what? Male leads? Directors? Producers?

He wondered what she'd think if she knew that Greg Reynolds was sitting at the back of the theater, watching her. Then he snorted softly. She was too young. She probably didn't know who in the hell Greg Reynolds was! And besides, he reminded himself, it wasn't Greg Reynolds who sat unnoticed. It was Garrick Rodenhiser, and unnoticed was precisely what he wanted to be.

Shoving himself up from his chair, he strode quickly out of the theater.

But he was back several days later, sitting in the same seat, watching a rehearsal that had benefited from those several days' practice and become more refined. The best of the performers were clearly emerging—the strong ones distinguishing themselves from the weak as the director focused her coaching more and more on the latter. He watched for a while longer, not quite sure why he stayed, knowing that he didn't need the knot in his belly, that there were other things he'd rather be doing, but unable to move. At last he did move, and when he reached the fresh air, he felt a distinct sense of relief. Theaters were confining things, he decided.

Yet he went back again. A week later this time, and still not quite knowing why. But he was there. And this time he stayed in his seat until the rehearsal had ended and the performers, one by one, filed past him. The director was the last to leave, but while the others hadn't given him a glance as they'd passed, she stopped.

She was a pretty woman, Garrick noticed, viewing her up close for the first time. Tall and willowy, she had long brown hair that was pulled into a high clasp at her crown, only to tumble smoothly down from there. She wore jeans and a heavy jacket and was clutching an armload of papers to her chest. She was younger than he'd expected, perhaps in her mid-twenties; he guessed her to be either a teaching assistant or a graduate student.

"I've seen you here before," she said, cocking her head.

Garrick remained sprawled in his seat. "I've stopped by a few times."

"We'll be doing the show next weekend. I'd think you'd rather see it then."

"Rehearsals are more interesting. They allow you to see what really goes into the production."

"Are you a student of the theater?"

He took in a breath and pushed himself straighter. "Not exactly."

"A connoisseur?"

He shrugged, then hoisted himself to his feet. He didn't miss the slight widening of the woman's eyes at his height. "Not exactly. What about you?"

"A grad student. We often direct undergraduate productions." When she turned and started walking toward the door, he followed. His heart was pounding in protest, but his legs seemed not to hear.

"Doing Chekov is an ambitious endeavor," he remarked.

"Isn't that what learning is about—challenge?"

He didn't answer that. He'd never associated the acting he'd done with learning, and his major challenge had been in topping the Nielsens for the week. "Do you get much of a crowd at your shows?" he asked.

"Sometimes yes, sometimes no. This one probably won't be as well attended, since it's more serious and heavy. We'll get some of the university types, but the local crowd is drawn to lighter things." They'd passed through the lobby and reached the door, which Garrick held open with a rigid hand. As she stepped into the daylight, she looked up at him. "Do you live locally?"

"For now."

"Are you affiliated with the university?"

"I'm taking a few courses."

They'd stopped at the top of the stone steps. She was staring at him. "Studying anything special?"

"Latin."

She laughed. "That's an odd one." But her laughter died quickly. Her eyes were fixed on his. She frowned for an instant.

"Is something wrong?"

"Uh, no. You look vaguely familiar. I, uh, I don't think I know any Latin students."

He didn't know if it was a come-on. Yes, he thought her attractive, but it was an objective judgment. She didn't turn him on in any way, shape or fashion. Still, he didn't leave.

"Is this your first year here?" she asked as she continued to study him closely.

"Yes." Feeling inexplicably bold despite the damp palms he pressed to the insides of his pockets, he returned her gaze unwaveringly.

"Are you a professional student?"

"Nope."

"What did you do before you came here?"

"Work."

"Doing…?"

"I work up north."

Again she frowned. Her gaze fell to his beard, then returned to his eyes. "I'm really sorry, but you do look familiar."

"Maybe I just look like someone else," he suggested with an outer calm that was far from matched inside.

She started to shake her head, but paused. "That may be it." Her eyes sharpened; Garrick noticed that they were brown, rather nondescript, nowhere near as warm or interesting as Leah's gray ones. Then she grinned. "That *is* it. Has anyone ever told you that you look like Pagen?"

"Pagen?"

"You know, the guy on television a few years back? Actually, his name was Greg Reynolds. I was a teenager when Pagen was in his heyday. He was one beautiful man." She blushed, then frowned again. "He disappeared from the scene pretty quickly after the series ended. I wonder what happened to him."

"Maybe he left the business and went to live in the woods," Garrick heard himself say.

"Maybe," she mused, then her look grew skeptical. "Are you sure you're not him?"

Of course I'm not, Garrick could have said, or *Are you kidding?* or *No way!* Instead, and for reasons unknown to him, he shrugged.

"You are," she said, an inkling of excitement in her voice. "You are Greg Reynolds. I can see it now. Your hair's a little different and you have a beard, but the eyes are the same…and the mouth." She was looking at the last in a way that made him press it closed.

"You're not talking," she announced with a sage nod, then held up one hand. "And your secret's safe with me. I promise." Then, suddenly, all pretense of maturity crumbled. "I don't believe it's you," she singsonged, eyes aglitter. "What was it like in Hollywood? It must have been so exciting doing the series! I thought you were wonderful! I'd like to be there for one day—one week—one month! You really *made* it. What have you done since then? Have you ever considered doing something here? You can't have retired from acting completely, not after…all that!"

"I've retired," he said quietly, but the statement was ineffective in staunching her enthusiasm.

"I had no idea we had a celebrity in our midst. No one else did, either, or word would have spread. My students would *love* to meet you. You'd be an inspiration!"

He shook his head. "I think not." He took a step to leave, but she put a hand on his sleeve.

"Maybe you'd speak before the theater group. I know the other grad students and the professors would be as excited as I am—"

"Thank you, but I really can't."

When he started off, she fell into step beside him. "Just me, then. Would you let me take you to lunch some day? You have no idea how much I'd like to hear about your experiences. God, they'd make a fantastic book. Have you ever thought of writing about your years as Pagen?"

"No," he said, and quickened his step.

"How about it? Just lunch, or...or dinner? I know a fantastic little place that's dark and quiet. No one would have to know we were there—"

"I'm really not free." He strode on.

The young woman stopped, but she couldn't resist calling after him. "Mr. Reynolds?"

He didn't answer. He wasn't Mr. Reynolds. Not anymore.

The night, while he and Leah were finishing off the last of the stew he'd made, Garrick told her what had happened.

"You told her who you were?" Leah asked in astonishment. It was the last thing she'd have expected him to do.

"She guessed, and I didn't deny it." He was reclining in his chair, one arm hooked over its back, the other fiddling absently with the spoon he hadn't used. He looked nearly as confused as Leah. "It was strange. I think I wanted her to know, but for the life of me I can't understand why. You know how I feel about my anonymity." He looked up, those wonderful hazel-and-silver eyes clouded. "Why did I do that, Leah?"

"I'm not sure," she answered quietly. "Did you feel anything…sitting there in the theater?"

"It was interesting. The kids were pretty good. But did I feel envious? No."

"Did you get the urge to jump up there?"

"God, no."

"You didn't miss being on center stage?"

"I didn't miss being on stage period. I was very happy to be sitting in the dark."

She breathed a tiny sigh of relief.

"I heard that," Garrick chided, narrowing one eye. "You were worried."

"I don't want you to miss anything about that life," she said a little evasively, then added, "What about the woman?"

"What about her?"

"Do you think that somehow, maybe subconsciously, you wanted to impress her?"

He shook his head. "No. She was pretty and all, but not like you."

"But she's a thespian."

"Good word, but it has no relevance."

"Sure it does. She's involved in the same kind of life you came from. A person like that might not go gaga over trapping, but she would about acting, particularly big-time acting."

"What I used to do was small time compared to the people who do Chekov or Williams or—even more so—Shakespeare. No, I wasn't trying to impress her."

"Maybe you just got tired of the waiting."

"What do you mean?"

Leah searched for an example to illustrate her point. The only one was the most obvious, and since it filled so much of her thoughts, she went with it. "There are times," she began quietly, "when I just want this baby to be born—one way or the other. It's the waiting and worrying and not knowing that's so bad. Even if the worst happens, at least I'll know, so I can go on with my life."

"Leah…"

"I'm sorry, but it's the only thing I can think of, and it makes my point. I would assume that for you, it must be nearly as bad wandering around Concord, waiting for someone to recognize you, worrying about what will happen when someone does. Maybe you wanted to get it over with. Maybe one part of you wanted that woman to know who you were."

He opened his mouth to protest, then clamped it shut and was silent for a minute. "Maybe."

"How did you feel when the truth came out?"

His tawny brows knit as he tried to verbalize his thoughts. "Weird. A little proud, but a little like an imposter, too. I felt distanced…like she was talking about someone else entirely when she started bombarding me with questions. I felt like I was playing a game, letting her *believe* I was Greg Reynolds, superstar, when I knew that I wasn't."

"Did she bring back memories of how the fans used to be?"

"Yes and no. She went all wide-eyed and high-voiced like a typical fan, but I didn't like it the way I used to. To tell you the truth, it was disgusting. Up to that point, she'd seemed dignified." He gave a lopsided grin. "I have to admit that I felt damn good walking away from her."

"Do you think she was offended?"

"Lord, I hope so," he answered without remorse. "With luck, she'll dismiss me as a fraud. If she starts blabbing about who I am, things might get a little hairy."

"She doesn't know your real name."

He scowled. "No, but she knows I'm studying Latin. It wouldn't be hard for her to track me down. Maybe I'll cut the next class or two and stay here with you."

"Chicken."

"Nuh-uh." He covered her hand with his and began a gentle massage. "I do want to be here with you. It's getting close."

"Three weeks."

"How do you feel?"

"Tired."

"Emotionally?"

"Tired. I meant what I said before. The waiting's getting to me."

"Everything's been fine so far."

"It was the other two times, too."

"You've never had a cesarean section before. It'll minimize stress on the baby during delivery."

"I hope."

He squeezed her hand. "It will. Things will work out fine, love. You'll see. A month from now, we'll have a squirming little thing on our hands."

"That's just what I told myself eight months into two other pregnancies."

"But this time is different. That's *my* baby you're carrying."

She sighed, then smiled sadly. "Which is precisely why I want it so badly."

The next week was an uneventful one for Leah, but, then, she'd known it would be. Aside from when she was eating or using the bathroom, she remained in bed. She didn't do much reading because she couldn't seem to concentrate. She didn't do much weaving because, with the bulk of the loom and that of her stomach, she couldn't get comfortable. She listened to music, which was fine for a time, particularly since Garrick kept her supplied with new tapes that they both enjoyed. Susan came to visit often, usually—and deliberately, Leah suspected, to keep an eye on her—while Garrick was in school.

She didn't do much work of the official puzzle-making variety because she'd declared herself on a temporary leave of absence. But she found herself working on that private puzzle, the one involving words that related to what she'd fondly come to think of as the life and times of Garrick and Leah. It was a whimsical endeavor and it helped keep her occupied.

Garrick's week wasn't quite as uneventful. He went back to school without missing a class, and though he was edgy during the first two days, he saw no sign of the young woman from the theater. On the third day, just when he was beginning to relax again, she accosted him as he was leaving his class.

"I have to talk to you for a minute, Mr. Reynolds," she said quickly and a little nervously as she fell into step beside him. "I was serious about what I said the other day. It would mean the world to all of us if you would agree to speak."

He kept walking at the same even pace. "I have nothing to say."

"But you do. You've had experiences we've only dreamed of having."

"I'm not who you think I am."

"You are. After we talked the other day, I went to the library and pored through the microfilms. The last anyone heard from or saw of Greg Reynolds was shortly before an automobile accident. The accident was reported in the papers. Greg Reynolds survived it, then disappeared. With your face and body, it would be too much of a coincidence to think that you're not him."

He sliced her a glance, but she went on, clearly proud of herself.

"I researched further. Greg Reynolds's real name is Garrick Rodenhiser. That's the name you've enrolled under here."

Garrick stopped then. "I'm a private citizen, Miss—"

"Schumacher. Liza Schumacher."

"I don't give talks, Miss Schumacher—"

"Liza. We could keep it to a small group, if that's what you'd prefer."

"I'd prefer," he said quietly, almost beseechingly, "to have my privacy respected."

"We'd pay you—"

"No, thanks." He started off again.

"An hour. A *half*-hour. That's all we'd ask—"

But he simply shook his head and kept going. Fortunately she didn't follow.

Again he told Leah about the encounter. Again she explored his feelings about it. "Are you sure you don't want to do it?"

"Speak? Are you kidding?"

"She's right, in a way. You have had the kind of experience that many of them want. It's not unusual for representatives of different careers to talk to groups of students."

"Whose side are you on, Leah?"

"Yours. You know that."

Thrusting his legs from the bed, he landed on his feet and stalked off to the window. "Well, I don't want to speak—before students or any other group. For one thing, I don't think much of the kind of experience I had. For another, I don't relish the idea of confessing my sins to an audience."

"There was a positive side to what you did."

"Mmm. Somewhere. I can't seem to see it, though. I suppose I could make up a good story...."

"Garrick..."

He continued to stare out the window.

"Why—really—won't you speak?"

He was silent for several more minutes, but he knew that Leah suspected the truth. It remained to be seen whether he had the courage to confirm it.

"Ah, hell," he muttered at last. "The truth of it is that deep down inside, I'm afraid I'll like the feeling of power that comes when you've got an audience in your thrall—the rapt faces, the adulation, the applause. If I do it once, I may want to do it again, and if I do it a second time, a third could follow, and by that time I could be hooked on how wonderful I am."

"You are wonderful."

He bent his head and smiled, then turned and re-traced his steps to the bed. Stretching out on his stomach before Leah, he grabbed her hand and pressed it to her lips. "You're the only one I want to hear saying that, because you're the only one who knows the real me. I've never talked to anyone the way I have to you. You're better than an analyst any day."

Leah wasn't sure if she liked the idea of being an analyst, because knowing another person's thoughts meant knowing his fears, and Garrick still had many. She thought he'd made progress since he'd been in Concord, and perhaps, to some extent, he had—but he still didn't trust himself. And that frightened her. She knew that she'd need his strength in the coming weeks and she didn't want anything to dilute it.

"I'll settle for being your soul mate," she said, and offered her lips for a kiss.

The sudden snowstorm that hit during the first week of December did nothing for Leah's peace of mind. True, Garrick's classes were canceled, so he stayed home with her. But she had visions of going into premature labor while they were snowbound, in which case everything they'd gone through might have been in vain.

They weren't truly snowbound, as it happened. Nor did she go into premature labor. Day by day, though, she felt the baby move lower, and though Gregory had made arrangements to do the section on the fifteenth of December, she wondered if Garrick's monster would wait that long.

It was harder to see Garrick off to class now. She was physically uncomfortable and emotionally strung out. Only when he was with her could she begin to relax, knowing that he'd take over if something happened. But she did send him off. She felt he needed it, in more respects than the obvious one of taking his mind off the baby and her.

On the eleventh of December she wished she'd been more selfish.

10

Garrick left class and walked to his car, but he'd barely reached for the door, when a loud call echoed across the parking lot.

"Mr. Reynolds!"

His grip tightened on the handle. Only one person would call him that, and the last thing he wanted to do was to talk with her now. He wanted to be home with Leah.

"Mr. Reynolds! Wait! Please!"

He opened the door and fleetingly contemplated jumping inside, slamming down the locks and wheeling off. But he wasn't a coward. Not anymore.

Propping one arm above the window, he turned his head toward the young woman approaching. "Yes, Miss Schumacher?"

Breathing hard from the run, she skidded to a halt by his side. "Thank you for waiting…I wanted to get here earlier…my class ran late."

"I'm running late myself. Was there something you wanted?" His breath was a white cloud in the cold air, though not quite large enough for him to vanish into as he wished he could do.

"Since you didn't feel comfortable speaking, I had another idea." She darted a quick glance behind her. To Garrick's dismay, a young man was trotting up to join them. "Darryl's with the town newspaper. I thought— we thought—that it would be super to have an article…."

Garrick frowned. "I thought you said this would be our secret."

"I did. But then I started thinking." She was slowly catching her breath. "It didn't seem fair to be selfish—"

"About what?"

"About knowing who you are. It seemed unfair that I should keep everything to myself—"

"Unfair to *you?*"

"No, no. To the people around here who would find your story interesting."

Garrick studied her steadily. "What about me? What about what's fair and unfair where *I'm* concerned?"

If anything, she grew bolder. "You're a star, Mr. Reynolds. Doesn't that bring with it certain responsibilities?"

"I'm not a star anymore," he stated unequivocally and with an odd kind of pride. "I'm a private citizen. I have many responsibilities, but as far as I can see, none of them have to do with you, or your fellow students, or your professors, or your friends." He cocked his head toward the reporter. "Is he your boyfriend?"

She exchanged an awkward look with Darryl. "We've gone out a few times, but that doesn't have anything—"

"Are you lovers?"

"That's not—"

"Is she good?" Garrick asked Darryl.

Liza went red in the face. "That's none of your business. I don't see what my private life has to do with—"

"*My* private life?" Garrick finished. "Nothing, Miss Schumacher. My questions are as much an invasion of your privacy as anything you—or Darryl—would ask *me*. I've already told you that I'm not interested in appearing publicly. That goes for big talks, small talks, newspaper articles and whatever *else* you come up with."

While he'd been speaking, Liza's expression had gone from embarrassment to dismay. In the silent minute that followed, it moved to anger. "The papers I read were right," she decided, abandoning all pretense of deference. "You are arrogant."

"Not really," Garrick said, surprised by the feeling of peace that was settling over him. "I"m simply trying to explain my feelings." And not only to her. Suddenly things were falling into place. His vision of who he was and what he wanted in life was becoming crystal clear.

Liza drew herself straighter. "I think you're a has-been. You disappeared from the acting scene. I think it was because you couldn't land any good parts after *Pagen*. I think you're afraid to stand before a group, knowing that."

She was tall, but Garrick was taller. Setting his shoulders back, he took a deep breath. "You know something, Miss Schumacher? I don't care what you think. The fact of the matter is that I'm not afraid to stand before anyone. I'm simply…not…interested. I chose to give up acting because it did nothing good for my life. You could offer me top billing in your next production and I'd refuse. You could offer to let me direct and I'd refuse. You could offer me headlines in the paper and I'd refuse. I live quietly now. I have a life that is much richer than anything I've known before. If you'd like to do an article, I'd be happy to tell you about trapping, or studying Latin, or whittling chess sets. As for acting, it's not *me* anymore. I've been away from it for nearly five years now, and I don't miss it."

"I find that hard to believe," Liza said.

"I'm sorry."

"You're satisfied being a…a trapper?"

"That's only one of the things I do, but, yes, I'm satisfied. Very satisfied."

"But the publicity—"

"Means nothing to me. I don't need it, and I don't want it." His tone was a mellow one, but it held undisputable conviction, just as the glance he sent Darryl held more sympathy than apology. "I'm sorry you won't get your story, but I really have nothing more to say."

"Mr. Rodenhiser? Mr. Rodenhiser!"

His head shot up in response to the alarmed cry, eyes flying in the direction of the voice. It came from a woman he recognized as being a secretary in the language department. She was clutching a coat around her with one hand, waving a small piece of paper in the other as she speed-walked toward the car.

"Thank goodness you haven't left," she panted.

The sense of peace Garrick had experienced earlier was gone. His blood ran cold.

"You just received a call from a Susan Walsh. She said that you were to meet Leah at the hospital."

"Oh, God," he whispered hoarsely, but the words hadn't left his mouth before he was in the car, leaving Liza Schumacher to jump out of the way of the slamming door. She and her boyfriend, the secretary, the school, the newspaper—all were forgotten. The only things he could think of were Leah and their baby. *What had happened?*

Over and over he asked the question, sometimes silently, sometimes aloud. He drove as fast as he could, swerving after what seemed an eternity into a space outside the hospital's emergency entrance. After being directed from one desk to the next, he finally connected with Gregory, who quickly put a reassuring arm around his shoulder.

"Her water broke. We're prepping her now. Come on. We'll both scrub up."

"How is she?"

"Terrified."

"And the baby?"

"So far, so good. I want to take it as quickly as possible."

Garrick didn't ask any more questions. He was too busy praying. Besides, he knew that Gregory didn't have the answer to the one question he most wanted to ask. Only time would give that, and time was precious. He matched his step to the doctor's as they hurried down the hall.

Leah's eyes were on the door when Garrick entered the delivery room. She held out a shaking hand and clutched his fingers fiercely. "They said you were on your way. Thank God you're here."

"What happened?"

"My water broke. I was lying in bed and it just broke. I hadn't moved, I hadn't done anything—"

"Shhhh." He was bending over her, pressing his mouth to her matted bangs. "You've done everything right, Leah. You've followed doctor's orders to the letter. Tell me, how did you get here?"

"I called Susan. Wasn't that stupid? I should have called Gregory directly, but I remember thinking that Susan was closer and that I was glad we had a phone so I wouldn't have to walk from the apartment to the house."

"It was smart of you to call Susan. She's cool under fire."

"She called Gregory, and Gregory called the ambulance while I just sat there, *trembling*."

"It's okay, honey." He had a hand in her hair but was looking around the room in bewilderment, trying to interpret every nuance of the bustling activity. "Everything's going to be okay." A cloth barrier was being lifted into place to shield the operation from their view. He knew that it was standard procedure for a cesarean section, but then it struck him that, since her water had broken, she had to be in labor. His eyes shot to hers. "Are you in pain?"

She gave a rapid little shake of her head. "I felt a few contractions before, but the spinal's taken effect. I don't feel a thing." Her eyes widened and her fingers tightened around his. "I don't feel anything, Garrick. Maybe something's happened—"

Gregory came up at that moment. "The baby's fine, Leah. We're monitoring the heartbeat, and it's fine."

His gaze swung from her face to Garrick's, then back. "All set to go?"

Their nods were identically jerky. Gregory moved off. The anesthetist came to sit by Leah's head, while a nurse slid a stool beneath Garrick.

"Please, let it live," Leah whispered to no one in the room.

"It will," Garrick whispered back, but his eyes were worried as they sought out Gregory.

"We're all thinking positive," was Gregory's response. He wasn't making promises, but he appeared fully confident, which was as much as Leah could have asked.

"Garrick?" she murmured.

"Yes, love?"

"How did everything go at school today?"

He was momentarily startled. His thoughts weren't on school. It was an unlikely subject to discuss given the time, place and circumstance. But he quickly understood what Leah was doing, so he forced himself to shift gears. "Not bad. I aced the exam."

"No kidding?"

His smile was wobbly. "Would I kid at a time like this? I got a ninety-seven."

"They say that older students do better."

"And I aced something else today."

"What?"

"Liza Schumacher."

They were talking in hushed tones, eyes locked into each other's with an urgency that acknowledged something momentous was taking place.

"What happened with Liza Schumacher?" Leah asked.

"She approached me with a local journalist in tow."

"Journalist!"

"They wanted an interview."

"Oh, no." Her fingers tightened around Garrick's, but it didn't have to do with the interview as much as the quiet talk coming from beyond the cloth barrier. She wanted to ask what was happening but didn't dare.

Garrick seemed in a similar quandary. He darted frantic eyes toward Gregory, who was concentrating on his work, his lower face covered by a mask. Garrick quickly calmed his expression when he looked down at Leah again.

"I said that I wasn't interested and it struck me that I wasn't. I really wasn't."

"Temptation—"

"Isn't temptation. I don't want what's being offered. There's nothing to threaten me."

"But if she'd already told one reporter who you are—"

"It doesn't matter. She can tell ten reporters, and it still won't matter."

"And if this one reporter writes something—"

"That's fine. He can write about how I've found a better life. It's not the kind of story that will sell papers, so one installment will be enough. He'll lose interest. Other reporters will, too. And it won't bother me at all."

"I'm glad," she whispered, then added quickly, "What are they doing?"

"Baby's doing well, Leah," came Gregory's call. "You two keep talking. It sounds like a fascinating discussion."

"I want the baby, Garrick," she whimpered.

"Me, too, love. Me, too. Are you feeling anything?"

"No."

"Any pain?"

"No."

All too aware of the emotional pain she was undergoing, he sent a panicky glance toward the anesthesiologist. "Maybe you should have knocked her out."

"No!" Leah cried. "I want to know."

"We're getting there, Leah," came Gregory's utterly calm voice.

It settled Leah momentarily. Tipping her head farther toward Garrick, she pressed their twined hands to her warm cheek. "When…when are finals?" she asked in the same small whisper she'd used before.

"Another week. I may skip them."

"Oh, no—after all the work you've done?"

"I'm only taking the courses for fun."

"Then take the exams for fun."

"Exams aren't fun."

"I'll help you study."

"That might be fun. But then you might be—"

A tiny cry cut off his words. His heart began to slam against his ribs, and he jerked up his head.

Leah's breath was catching in her throat. "Garrick?" She raised her voice. "Gregory?"

Another stronger cry echoed through the room, followed by Gregory's satisfied, "Ahhh, she's a lusty one."

"She," Leah breathed, tear-filled eyes clinging to Garrick's face.

He was rising from the stool, tearing his gaze from

Leah to focus on the small bundle Gregory held. A tiny arm flailed the air. Grinning through unchecked tears, he returned to Leah.

"She waved."

"She's moving?"

"See for yourself," said Gregory as he held the baby high.

Leah saw. Arms and legs batted the air to the tune of a sturdy pair of lungs. Leah started to cry, too. "She's... alive...beautiful...Garrick...do you...see?"

He had an arm curved around Leah's head. "I see," he managed to croak, then pressed his wet cheek to her forehead.

"Show's over," came the decree from the pediatric specialist who'd been assisting in the proceedings. He gently took the infant from Gregory. "Sorry, folks. She's mine for a few minutes."

It was just as well. Leah's arms were around Garrick's neck, and they were burying their faces against each other, muffling soft sobs of gratitude and joy.

"Amanda Beth. It's as beautiful as she is." Leah was lying flat in bed, per doctor's orders, but Garrick was sitting by her side, so she didn't mind the temporary restriction.

Garrick's face was alight with pride. "The pediatrician can't find a thing wrong with her. They'll keep a close watch on her for a few days, but they don't foresee any problem."

"Seven pounds, five ounces."

"Not bad for an early baby."

"Oh, Garrick, I'm so happy!" She was smiling

broadly, as was Garrick, neither of them able—or caring—to stop.

"We did it. *You* did it. Thank you, Leah. Thank you for giving me a beautiful daughter, and for giving me self-confidence, and for loving me."

Grabbing his ear, she tugged him down for a kiss. "Thank *you.* I feel so complete."

"That's good," he said, raising his head a trifle. "Because we're expecting visitors in a few minutes, and I want you at your best."

"Victoria?" she asked in excitement.

"Nope. She'll be here later in the week. Insists on helping you out when we take baby home."

Her smile grew dreamy. "Take baby home. I never thought we'd be saying those words." For the first time her smile faltered. Her eyes went wide behind her glasses. "Garrick! Clothes, diapers, a crib—we haven't got *anything!*" After two pregnancies when she'd been fully equipped, only to find herself without a baby, she'd been superstitious.

Garrick was unfazed. "No sweat. I'll pick up a crib—I think maybe a cradle—tomorrow. Victoria's buying the rest."

"Victoria? But she can't—"

He arched a brow. "Victoria?"

"Well, she can, but we can't let her!"

"I'm afraid we can't stop her. She was in a rush to get off the phone so that she could get to the stores before they closed."

Leah was smiling again. "That does sound like Victoria."

"She feels responsible for the baby," he said, eyes twinkling.

"Maybe we should let her think she is. We couldn't very well make her interrupt her shopping to research the facts of life, could we?"

He kissed her nose. "Certainly not."

"Garrick?"

But it wasn't Garrick who answered. "Hello, hello" came Susan's singsong voice from the door. Gregory was wheeling her in, followed closely by a man Leah had never seen before.

"Ah. Our visitors." Garrick stood up quickly, kissing Susan, shaking hands with Gregory, then with the other man, whom he brought forward. "Leah, say hello to Judge Hopkins. He's agreed to marry us."

"Marry us?" Leah cried. "But...but I can't get married now!"

"Why not?"

"I...because I look a mess! My hair's tangled and I'm sweaty—"

"But you are wearing white," Garrick pointed out in a mischievous tone.

"A hospital gown," Leah returned in dismay. "They won't even let me sit up to change."

"No problem," said Susan as she tugged a box from where it had been stowed between her hip and the chair. She turned to the men as a group. "Out." Then to her husband. "Be a sweet and send a nurse in here to give us a hand." Then to the judge. "We'll only be a minute, Andrew." Then to Garrick. "Think you can control yourself that long?"

None of them answered, because Gregory was busy pushing them toward the door.

Leah was married in the gown and matching robe that Susan had somehow known to buy in pale pink. Garrick, wearing the same sweater and cords he'd worn to school that day, stood by her bedside, holding her hand, while the judge conducted the brief ceremony. When, at its conclusion, Gregory produced a bottle of champagne, Leah threw an apprehensive look at Garrick, who leaned low and spoke for her ears alone.

"You can't have any for another few hours, but then we'll share a little. Just a sip in token celebration. I don't need any more of a high than the one I'm on now. I don't think I ever will."

Five days later, Garrick and Leah brought Amanda Beth back to the small garage apartment. Leah was healing well, and the baby was as strong and healthy as they'd prayed she would be.

Victoria, who was staying in the Walsh's main house, was in her element. Declaring that Amanda was more interesting than the Maori any day, she fought Garrick for the honor of bathing, diapering and dressing her.

Since Leah was nursing, the feeding chores were hers alone. She loved those times when Amanda was suckling and the rest of the world became a warm, fuzzy periphery. Even more, though, she loved the times at night when Garrick would stretch out beside her and watch.

"What does it feel like?"

"When she nurses?"

"Mmm. Does it hurt?"

"Oh, no! It's a delightful kind of gentle tugging."

"Like when I kiss you there?" He drew a light fore-finger across the upper swell of her breast.

"A little. There's a sense of depth. I feel like there are strings inside me that she's pulling on. Sometimes I feel contractions. But it's different, too."

"How?"

"When she does it, it's satisfying in and of itself. When you do it, it makes me want more." She blushed. "Different kinds of sensations."

Garrick moaned and shifted his legs, making no attempt to hide his problem. The light in the eyes he raised to hers wasn't one of uncontrollable desire, though, as much as love. "I can't conceive of life without you, Leah. You...Amanda...when I think of the sterile existence I had before..."

"Don't look back," she urged in a whisper as she bent forward and brushed his lips with hers. "We've conquered the past. We have a wonderful present. Let's look forward to the future for a change."

They did just that. After long discussions with Leah, Garrick decided that he rather liked the idea of working toward the college degree he'd never earned. Baby and all, he managed to study for and do well in his finals, paving the way for his acceptance at Dartmouth, which had an excellent Latin department.

"You'll love Hanover," he told Leah. "It's got charm."

"I know I'll love it, but what about you? Don't you miss the cabin?"

"To tell you the truth, no." He seemed as surprised as she that the answer came so quickly. "I love it up there, but my life now is so full that I rarely think of it. I'd like to get a house in Hanover and use the cabin as a vacation retreat."

That was exactly what they did. With Amanda strapped into a carrier against Garrick's chest, they looked at every possible home in Hanover, finally falling in love with and buying a small Victorian within walking distance of Garrick's classes. During school vacations, weather permitting, they returned to the cabin. Come June, shortly before they were to retreat there for the summer, Garrick approached Leah with a proposal.

"How about a trip to New York?"

Her eyes lit up. "New York?"

"Yeah. I know you hated it last time you went—"

"I was pregnant and tired and worried, and you weren't with me." Her voice lowered. "Will you go this time?"

"I won't let you and Amanda go alone, and Victoria has been begging us for months to visit."

She wrapped an arm around his waist. "I'd love to go, Garrick, but only if you're sure."

"I'm sure." He winked down at her. "We may even be able to get some time to ourselves."

Their visit to New York was enlightening in several respects. Garrick found that he was relaxed and at ease. Leah found that though they had a wonderful time, she was ready to leave again when the time came.

Equally as gratifying was Victoria's news. She'd heard through the grapevine that Richard and his wife had had a second baby—this one stillborn. And while Leah's heart went out to them, she couldn't help but close her eyes in relief. It seemed that Richard's wife, not about to take the tragedy sitting down, had done some research. Richard had been adopted at birth, but she'd managed to work through the courts to determine his biological parents—and had discovered that infant mortality had been documented over two generations on his father's side.

"All our worrying was for nothing," Leah breathed, but Garrick was quick to disagree.

"No, love. The worry may have been unnecessary, but it served a purpose. If you hadn't been worried, you'd never have left me and moved to Concord. And if you hadn't done that, I would have stayed at the cabin, where I would be to this day. Think of all we'd have missed."

She knew that he was right. His self-confidence had been fully restored, and his self-respect had taken on new dimensions. He'd survived the auto accident and found a fresh basis for life, but only since Leah had come had he begun to really grow.

Which was what she wanted to do…again. "This means we can have another baby—"

"Without worry."

"But not just yet."

"Maybe when Amanda's two."

"We'll go for a boy this time."

"How're we gonna arrange that?"

"There are ways. I was reading an article recently that said—"

"Since when do you read articles about planning a baby's sex?"

"Since the world has opened up to me and I've begun to dream again."

* * *

Through the years to come, Leah and Garrick both did their share of dreaming, each time setting out to make those dreams come true. But during that first summer at the cabin with Amanda, they were too content to do much dreaming. The sun was warm, the air fresh, the forest as magnificent and lush as they'd ever seen it. Garrick worked in his garden, often with Amanda babbling in sweet baby talk beside him. Leah was always nearby, often constructing puzzles to send off to her editor. The crossword from which she took the most pleasure, though, was the one that chronicled the life and times of Leah and Garrick. Now there was Amanda to fit into the grid, but doing so was simple.

"Aha," Garrick teased. "So *that's* why you wanted to name her Amanda. Three *A*'s. You need them."

"I named her Amanda because I love the name and you love the name and because, obviously, *she* loves the name."

"She'd love *any* name, as long as there's banana ice cream after we call her."

"I love banana ice cream."

"So do I. But I love you and Amanda more. Hey—" he studied her puzzle "—have you got it here?"

"What?"

"Love."

"Sure. It's all over the place—in every noun, every adjective, every—"

"Four letters. L-O-V-E."

"It's there."

"I can't find it."

"Look closer."

"I can't find it."

"Look higher."

"I can't find it."

"To the right."

"I can't—I can. Ahhhh. There it is. Twelve across. L-O-V-E. Very simple and straight to the point. Now that's my kind of word."

New York Times bestselling author

BARBARA DELINSKY

presents four romantic titles that have become reader favorites.
Specially priced at $4.99 U.S./$5.99 CAN.

BARBARA DELINSKY

$4.99 U.S.
$5.99 CAN.

BARBARA DELINSKY

Could the love they shared be...

T.L.C.

The Outsider

BARBARA DELINSKY

Twelve Across

Sometimes love finds you, no matter how well you hide...

Available the first week of January 2006 wherever paperbacks are sold!

BARBARA DELINSKY

They couldn't change the past, but could they hold a future?

First, Best and Only

MIRA®

www.MIRABooks.com

MBDVP0106

New York Times bestselling author

DEBBIE MACOMBER

brings readers four of her classic novels of
finding hope, happiness and love.

**Specially priced
at $4.99 U.S./$5.99 CAN.**

$4.99 U.S.
────────
$5.99 CAN.

*Available
the first
week of
January 2006
wherever
paperbacks
are sold!*

www.MIRABooks.com

MDMVP010

The final book in
the breathtaking
Bride's Necklace
trilogy by
New York Times
bestselling author

Kat Martin

Trying to win back the trust of his jilted love, Rafael,
Duke of Sheffield, presents her with a stunning necklace
rumored to hold great power. As much as Dani wants
to believe it can right the wrongs of the past, she fears
there is one truth it cannot conceal, a truth that could
cost her this second chance with Rafe, the only man she
has ever loved....

The Handmaiden's Necklace

"Kat Martin is one of the best authors around!
She has an incredible gift for writing."
—*Literary Times*

*Available the first week of January 2006
wherever paperbacks are sold!*

MIRA®

www.MIRABooks.com   MKM2207

MIRA®

New York Times bestselling author

JENNIFER BLAKE

Lisette Moisant is a widow, courtesy of the swordsmanship of Caid O'Neill. He bested her loathsome husband in a duel, but now she is a target for schemers who wish to steal her fortune and see her dead. It is Caid to whom she turns for protection, and guilt leaves him no recourse but to agree to Lisette's request.

But soon New Orleans is flooded with rumors, suggesting the two plotted to kill Lisette's husband all along. In a society where reputation is everything, the scandal threatens Lisette and Caid with ruin…and the person responsible will stop at nothing until they have paid with their lives.

Dawn Encounter

"The first in Blake's new series evokes everything alluring about New Orleans."
—*Romantic Times BOOKclub* on *Challenge to Honor*

Available the first week of January 2006 wherever paperbacks are sold!

www.MIRABooks.com

MJB2213

Award-winning author

Gloria Goldreich

**"And the worst of it is, you understand,
that I can't leave him:
there are the children, and I am bound.
Yet I can't live with him...."**

The words from Anna Karenina resonate with the women who have
gathered over good food and wine for their first book club meeting
of the year. These six very different women are not quite friends,
not quite strangers but, bonded by their love of literature, they
share a deep understanding of one another—or so they think.

DINNER WITH ANNA KARENINA

"In lyrical prose, Goldreich
offers a sad yet hopeful tale
of a woman whose personal
tragedy ultimately yields to
greater self-awareness and
deeper happiness."
—*Booklist* on
Walking Home

*Available the first week of
January 2006 wherever
hardcover books are sold!*

MIRA®

www.MIRABooks.com

MGG2227

LUANNE JONES

"No better than a pack of heathens." That's what their grandmother called Charma Deane, Bess and Minnie, three cousins growing up in rural Orla, Arkansas. To them, nothing could be better than being a heathen girl. But when Charma Deane is betrayed several times by her cousin Bess, she leaves Orla.

Now, years after leaving the "Aunt Farm" behind, Charma Deane's back to make peace with the past and repair the strained ties with Bess, and they remind each other of their old vow: live without limits, love without question, laugh without apologies and make sure that whoever dies first won't be sent to heaven looking like hell.

Heathen Girls

"Reading Luanne Jones is like an afternoon with a best friend. Lots of warmth, wicked wit and enough heart-wrenching honesty to keep things interesting."
—*New York Times* bestselling author Deborah Smith

*Available the first week of January 2006
wherever books are sold!*

MIRA®

www.MIRABooks.com   MLJ2282

A Dr. Morgan Snow novel

M. J. ROSE

The Scarlet Society is a secret club of twelve powerful and sexually adventurous women. But when a photograph of the body of one of the men they've recruited to dominate—strapped to a gurney, the number 1 inked on the sole of his foot—is sent to the *New York Times*, they are shocked and frightened. Unable to cope with the tragedy, the women turn to Dr. Morgan Snow. But what starts out as grief counseling quickly becomes a murder investigation, with any one of the twelve women a potential suspect.

THE
DELILAH COMPLEX

"A creepily elegant and sophisticated novel, with keen psychological insights. M. J. Rose is a bold, unflinching writer and her resolute honesty puts her in a class by herself."
—Laura Lippman

*Available the first week of January 2006
wherever paperbacks are sold!*

www.MIRABooks.com

MMR2215

THE CLASSIC GROUNDBREAKING
BLOCKBUSTER FROM
NEW YORK TIMES
BESTSELLING AUTHOR

ALEX KAVA

The brutal murders of three young boys paralyze the citizens of
Platte City, Nebraska. When FBI criminal profiler Maggie O'Dell
is called in to assist the case, she quickly pinpoints the true
nature of the evil behind the killings. And Maggie understands
something else: the killer is enjoying himself, relishing his ability
to stay one step ahead of her, making this case more personal
by the hour. Because out there, watching, is a killer with
a heart of pure and perfect evil.

A PERFECT
EVIL

"Alex Kava has created a suspenseful novel and
a winning character."—*Washington Post Book World*

Available the first week of January 2006 wherever paperbacks are sold!

www.MIRABooks.com   MAK2233